4

X

ARMED

=

A NOVEL
of the not so old west

by

Doug Ball

Front cover photo – the author

Back cover photo – the author

Other books by the author

Western adventures

Blood on the Zuni
Vengeance
Gentle Rebellion

State of Arizona series

State of Defense
State of Threat

Nonfiction

Puzzling Theology
The Fishy Prophet

Of course,
to
Patti

"Thrice is he armed who hath his quarrel just."
Shakespeare

"Four times is he armed, who gets his lick in 'fust'."
Josh Billings

"I turned from the perfume of the roses, from the white beauty of the lilies, from the din of the thronged streets, from the glare of the electric lights and from the conventionalities of the city life - and my mind went wandering away, to the land of the pungent odor of the wild sage and the balsam of the stately pine trees - to the starry stillness of the desert night and to the scarlet glory of the blossoming cactus, to the land of opportunity and hope - Arizona - the land where all men are bound together by brotherly sympathy - the land where the rich do not grind the faces of the poor, and the poor do not envy the splendor of the rich - Arizona - where, after the last scene is closed, and life's fitful dream is o'er, all her loyal sons and daughters will, on her bosom, find eternal peace and sweet repose."

Henry Fountain Ashurst

Senator from Arizona

Chapter 1

10 June 1980

It has been said Colonel Colt made men equal and Mr. Carnegie can teach you how to win friends and influence folks, but Juan Vasquez had always thought Messrs. Smith and Wesson gave a man the edge. If anybody needed an edge, it was Juan Vasquez.

Snuggling into the soft sand of the wash, he checked the loads in his Border Patrol model 41 Magnum for the umpteenth time. The dark brown slacks and tan shirt that covered his slight, just over five foot tall frame, bore none of the spit and polish of roll call that morning. His $200 Rezistol, "Deputy Special," hat lay in the dirt twenty feet away, shot to rags. Ten feet beyond the hat, his brass badge reflected the broiling late June sun up onto the open door of his disabled patrol car. One point of the star shaped badge pointed out a pair of buzzards circling overhead.

"If I ever get back to town, I can tell the Sheriff I found that son-of-a-mule with the 7mm Magnum," Juan continued his conversation with himself. "And, he can terminate my probation and I'll get started looking for a new job. Diamond C is hiring."

Another shot from the high-powered rifle slammed into the dirt of the wash bank, sending sand into the air, to settle, once again, on Juan's back.

Juan kept mumbling to himself. "A year ago, Wetback, the Sheriff said you'd charge Hell with a wet wash cloth and here you are hiding from a man with a rifle. Just because he's a good 150 yards away and all you got is a little bitty pistol with a little bitty shorty barrel, why should that stop you?" He answered himself with, "It's stopping you because that son took the radio antenna off the car with one shot. How's he gonna miss your scrawny butt if you stick it out? Crap! It'll be a good four hours or more before I'm missed, let alone anybody come out looking for me. That'll be tomorrow. Crap! They won't even know where to start looking."

Having only six months to go on the probation period before he got his permanent certification as a peace officer kept him walking on eggs. He had been fortunate enough to make a couple of good busts and had a letter of commendation in his record for saving a life. "But, losing a four-wheeler just might finish this career before it gets started," he thought. "I don't want to let Sheriff down after the way he stuck his neck out for me. Crap!"

The Sheriff had fought long and hard before the County Supervisors voted the monies for the off-road cars, and this one was near a total wipe out. It was going to need a new engine to go with cosmetic repairs to the body, and new glass all around.

"Who are you and why shoot at me?" he screamed for lack of something better to do.

The county's most wanted man let fly another round that poked another hole in the hood of the Burgundy Blazer.

"Crap!"

#

Billy Cranston had been foreman of Stirrup Ranch for more than ten years and had every intention of being foreman for many more years. He loved the feel of folks looking up to him as he walked through St. Johns. He was on his way to the Sheriff's office to report another crime.

Billy was also mad.

Miss Aggie could tell. He walked right past her without tipping his hat, and Billy Cranston tipped his hat to every woman, young or old, pretty to downright ugly. Miss Aggie might be a little past her prime, but she'd been downright beautiful in Billy's eyes when he'd started chasing her, years ago.

“Don't you say 'Hi' to old friends anymore, Billy Cranston?” Agatha Albright's voice could bite when she tried.

“Sorry, Aggie,” Billy pulled his hat from his head and turned to face her.

Standing on the open sidewalk with his hat in hand like a schoolboy, he added, “You know I'd never purposely pass you by without speaking, Aggie.”

“Yes, Billy. I know you wouldn't if you were thinking right. I was afraid you'd walk right into the street without looking and ruin somebody's shiny new truck.” The concern in her voice ruined the joke of her words.

“Thanks for lookin' out for the trucks of the folks hereabouts. I guess that ambusher is gettin' to me, Aggie. I can't think straight anymore. If I don't stop him soon, the boss is going to fire me and hire somebody who can.”

“Come on, Billy. This is 1980, not 1880. It's up to the law to get that person. That’s why we have a sheriff and a bunch of deputies.”

“Tell Handley that and we had a sheriff and a deputy in 1880.”

“I doubt if he'd listen. He hasn't listened to anybody since his daddy was killed.”

Bill chuckled a bit before saying, “Join me for lunch, Aggie?”

“I'd love to, Bill.”

“I'll meet you at the El Charro in thirty minutes, if you don't mind meeting me.”

“That'll be fine. You know, I never mind meeting you, Billy,” her voice as soft as a rabbit's fur, “but, you'll have to walk me home afterward, I’m done for the day.”

“Done.” His voice taking on a dreamy quality, he added, “I'd love to walk you home, Aggie. I have always loved walking you home.”

He put on his hat, “If you'll excuse me?” He turned and walked away without waiting for her answer.

#

Sheriff Beazley was laid back in his swivel chair with black cowboy boots that would have done a Marine proud firmly planted on the corner of the desk. Ben Beazley had been a Marine. He had been a Highway Patrolman, too. He'd done a lot of things before running for Sheriff. Now he was bored.

"What am I doing here? No challenge, no future, and I ain't getting any younger. Drunks and petty thieves get dull after fourteen years. The only excitement around here is some rustlers and that damned shooter out at the Stirrup. One's stealin' cows and the other's shootin' them," he thought.

"And, who gives a fat rat's patootie about cows?" he asked the wall.

"I do, and you had better care about them cows if you know what's good for you," Billy said, entering the office.

"Who in hell let you in here, Billy?"

"I let myself in here, and if you don't get up off you big fat backside and find out who's shooting up Stirrup, I may just run against you and make this my office, come next election."

"I wish you luck."

"I may just need the job, if something ain't done right quick."

"Sounds good to me, Billy. You can try to cover the 12,000 square miles of countryside in this county with thirteen underpaid deputies. Then you can solve the problem of jurisdiction on the reservations. When you think all that's taken care of, you can come up with a way to keep an eye on 70,000 head of stock with only 700 miles of paved roads to do it on and a trio of Supervisors who won't buy anything that flies and carries a man. They were goin' to get me a falcon once, but I found out they don't do too well as a witness in court."

"Right!"

"Now, what's so damned important you can't leave a report at the desk like everybody else and have to disturb me while I'm contemplating all the problems I just mentioned?" He pulled a cigar from his vest pocket while he was talking, and struck a match to it for punctuation.

"The man with the 7mm Magnum shot up another water tank, the windmill that fed it, and the eighteen cows standing around the drinker fed by it. The tank needs a dozen or so patches, the windmill needs a whole new top end, and we'll salvage the hides off the cows. Total loss is better than eighty-thousand bucks. One of them cows just happened to be a prize bull we paid a bundle for last month." Billy paused, and then added, "His brand hadn't even peeled."

"Look, Billy. I've got two of this meager force of deputies working full time on the 7mm shootings. I've asked the Governor for help. There just isn't a thing to go on. My best tracker - a court recognized expert, as you well know - loses all sign within half a mile of the shooting spot. If we ever find the rifle, we'll be able to match it to the couple a dozen cases and slugs we've got. When we find those size 9 1/2 boots, we'll match them to the six plaster casts down in the basement. I just can't guard Stirrup with my staff and the Supervisors aren't goin' to spring for more deputies in this county. This here county is broke, according to them."

"Maybe if somebody started shooting up the reservation, they'd get you the men."

"Most likely, Billy. Most likely."

"I know about all you're doin', but it ain't gettin' it done. Handley's goin' to have my hide nailed to the barn and then find another man for my job if something don't break pretty soon."

"What's he expect you to do, you ain't the law?"

"Don't ask me. I've hired six extra men, just to patrol the place. All the gates have nice, shiny, new locks on them. There ain't a spot on that ranch, all 360 square miles of it, that ain't seen at least twice a day. And, that's saying nothin' about two planes, one of which is in the air at all times during day. I'm at a loss. You're at a loss. So where does that leave us good guys?"

"Over a barrel, I guess."

"I don't much like that position."

"Let's go over to Lenny's and talk about it over a cold beer."

"You buy."

"Only the first one."

#

The brain behind the 7mm Magnum thought, “Two more rounds and I'll get out of here. Sure am glad I didn't nick Juan with that second shot, he's too good an hombre' to get hurt in this fight. He just keeps getting in the way.”

The gloved hands fed two more rounds into the Weatherby, cranked the variable powered scope up to twelve power and laid the polished stock alongside the right cheek. The eye lined up the cross hairs with the heel of Juan's boot, and the first finger of the right hand eased back on the trigger.

The heel came off the boot.

#

Miss Aggie walked into the café, found a seat in a booth, and waited for Maria to serve the coffee. She had fifteen minutes to wait, if Billy was on time.

He rarely was.

#

Juan Vasquez spit blood into the sand. The shock of the Magnum round hitting his boot heel caused him to bite his tongue. The way his foot was tingling, he didn't think he was going to play like the 7th Cavalry and charge the shooter.

“I'll get you and you better hope there's a bunch of witnesses around when I get my hands on you. You just think on where that rifle will end up, hombre,” he shouted at the wind.

The answer was prompt. Dust kicked up in his face just as the sound of the shot reached his ears. That shot coupled with the loss of his heel told him that all the rounds fired could have been put in his body instead of the dirt and the Blazer.

#

Silence reigned on the high desert, except for the cries of a pair of ravens in the distance, as the shooter started trotting away, thinking, “Next time, no more cows.”

#

Lenny's Place wasn't much of a tavern, but it served the purpose for St. Johns. It was the only place, inside the city limits, where a person could wet his or her whistle or dance to the country music from the jukebox.

More money changed hands in Lenny's and bigger deals were sealed there than any other place in the county. The safe behind the bar had been the only bank in town until a real bank set up business in 1962.

To go with the bar, Lenny wasn't much of a barkeeper, but he was the only one to ever work behind Lenny's bar. For three generations it had been the same. If Lenny was sick, the place was closed. If Lenny was indisposed, you just served yourself and left the money on the back bar in front to the register. The register was an old hand cranked, pop up number, antique that Lenny had been offered big money for many times. His answer was always the same, "Nope."

Lenny was in his usual spot behind the much scarred bar when the Sheriff and Billy walked in. He lifted two frosted glasses out of the chiller and set them under the tap. Pulling the ornate, wooden handle toward his chest, he said, "You two goin' to get drunk and raise a ruckus, you do it somewheres else. Otherwise, have a seat." He was smiling.

Billy and Ben had been friends for many a year, and in their younger days they had been known to take their fun fast and rowdy. It was common knowledge that when they couldn't find anybody else to fight, they'd chose up sides and square off against each other. The outcome was usually a draw, but occasionally one would best the other and they'd have to do it over again and again until the score was evened up.

The Sheriff hung his Stetson on the buffalo head at the end of the bar, slid out a stool, and sat. "Just serve the beer, Lenny. If we get too rowdy for you, you just call the law. City cops will come a runnin' fast enough." He, too, was smiling.

"Yeah, they'll come a runnin', but they'll probably join you two rather than break it up."

Billy got into the act with, "You sayin' my brother and cousin ain't handlin' their jobs proper, Lenny?"

Lenny placed the two glasses on the bar in front of the pair and said, “No, Billy, it's Ben's cousin I'm worried about, the Chief of them city boys don’t do much when it comes to Ben and his boys.” He picked up the bill the Sheriff had laid on the bar and added, “Glad to see ya, boys. Enjoy.”

“You coulda bought us one, Lenny. You didn't have to take my money, did ya?”

“Yeah, and have you arrest me for trying to bribe an Officer of the Law or call the alcohol boys on me for enticing-to-drink. Bull! You can buy like the rest of my customers.”

“Thanks, Lenny. Just keep the women off us for a while we got things to talk about.”

“Right!”

“Ben, I've got to get going and meet Aggie for lunch right soon, so let's get on with this. What are we gonna do about that shooter?”

“Other than what we've already done, it beats the heck out of me.” The Sheriff scratched his chin and stared into the mirror on the back bar. “In the six months this bum's been shooting up Stirrup, we haven't a clue as to who or why.”

“I keep waiting for him to start putting those slugs in people. I've had three hands quit on me, but there's always more cowboys looking for work than there are jobs in this neck of the woods. Them three were great hands and will be missed. I just wish whoever it is would let us know why or what he wants. Me, I think it's going to get worse before we find out what for.”

“You could be right, Billy. I think somebody's mad at Stirrup.” He looked Billy in the eye before continuing with, “You fired anybody lately?”

“Just that good-for-nothing Quince. He's been fired from every ranch around here at least once, and from Stirrup three times. He don't get mad, he gets drunk. I'll probably fire him four or five more times in the next few years, if he lives that long. When he works, he's the best.”

“So they tell me.” The Sheriff tipped his glass to get the dregs and added, “You buying?”

"Nope. I'm going to have lunch with Aggie. See you later, Ben." Bill headed for the door and Beazley signaled Lenny for another.

Lenny brought over a fresh, frosted glass filled from the tap, sat it on the counter, and pushed back the offered bill. "Keep it, Ben. I like the work you been doin'."

"Glad somebody does, Lenny. What with the shooter, rustlers, dopers, the tribe, and the Board of Supervisors, I don't know which is the biggest problem."

"Rustlers?"

"Yeah. Looks like we got a gang of them working the ranches. Signs of a big truck and motorcycles out by Miller's catch pens yesterday. Miller says he's missing at least forty head of steers he was planning on taking to the auction next week."

"That'll just about break him, won't it?"

"Not just about, it did break him. No insurance and the critters were mortgaged to the eyeballs. He gave up. The bank put his place on the market this morning. They're letting Miller stay on and manage the place for them until a new owner takes over. Even goin' to pay him. It'll probably be the first time Miller's ever made a nickel on that place."

"He was crazy for not having insurance, Ben. We've always had a few losses to rustlers on those absentee owner ranches." Lenny drew a beer for himself.

"Miller might have lived in town, but he spent more time on his spread than most of these quote ranchers unquote around here. Look at Evans. He goes out to his place once a month, whether he needs to or not. You'd think he would've learned two years ago when his well went dry. He damned near lost the whole herd. If them cows hadn't been smart enough to break through the fence he doesn't maintain and get to water at a Stirrup well, they would have died for sure. He's still mad at Chet for charging him so much for the water his cows drank."

The Sheriff took another swallow from his glass before going on. "We've always had some losses to rustling, sure, but it's been mostly people filling their freezers off a carcass or two, but this looks like well-organized pros. They've hit four places in the past two weeks."

"Let me get you another one. On the house, of course."

"Maybe if I get good and drunk, stagger down the street singing dirty ditties, they'll have a recall election and relieve me of all this." Ben chuckled as he killed the beer. "Nope, then I'd have to buy a car. One more's my limit, Lenny, and thanks."

#

Better than an hour had gone by since the last shot from the 7mm, Juan yelled.

Nothing.

He waved his hand.

Nothing.

He stood up.

No response.

Juan grabbed his well ventilated hat and slammed it on his head. He kicked his boot off and threw it into the scrub cedar behind him. The other cowboy boot followed the first into the scrub. Juan walked to the blazer and jerked out the spare boots he kept there. Jerking the laces tight, he thought on the months he'd kept the spare pair in the car to save wear and tear on his good boots. Now they would save his feet. Now he had a bit of dirt road stomping to do to get back to the highway. "Now and then you do something right, Wetback."

He tried the radio. He tossed the mike into the perforated Blazer and started the hike.

"Better than sixteen miles, Wetback. Crap. You better get to layin'em down and pickin'em up if you're going to make it by sundown." Talking to himself didn't make him feel any better, but he was the only soul there was to talk to and Juan Vasquez was a talking man.

"Crap."

#

Beer cans and soiled disposable diapers littered the road side as Lary Ronson drove toward his dream.

"Damn the bottle bills, let's get a diaper bill going. I can stand the rusting cans and broken glass, but the stench of those diapers is getting just a tad strong." He was talking to the dog sitting next to him.

The dog looked at Lary and appeared to smile.

"Crackers, you're a real companion. A good listener and a wet kiss when I get home, beats the living day lights out of that wife I used to keep around. You always know when to smile at my comments and when not to bother me. Never ran up the charge cards either, have ya? Oh, well, I guess I was as much or more at fault than she was for not making it work out. Failure just isn't fun, Crackers."

The beat up, mostly green, pickup rolled down the road while Lary whistled and chatted at the dog. Now and then, he'd scan his mirrors to check the road and load behind.

Lary was going back to the homestead his grandfather had proved up on sixty years ago. The homestead was a full section of land in Apache County, Arizona, thirty miles north and 20 miles west of the County Seat of St. Johns. "No more rat race of the city, just the peace and quiet of the country, a typewriter, and my dog," he kept thinking out loud.

Lary and Crackers made the left turn that marked the start of the 20 miles of unimproved roads to the homestead. The further they traveled from the pavement, the worse the road got, causing him to slow more and more to save the thin tires and worn suspension on the Chevy truck.

Lary was busy daydreaming of his new life as he rounded a tree. He locked up all four wheels, causing the truck to slew sideways in the sand. There was no gate where a gate should have been. There was just fence stretching as far as he could see in both directions. "This wasn't here nine years ago, Crackers."

The wire glistened in the afternoon sun, telling of its newness. The juniper posts ran with sap and green sprigs dangled. Hanging from the top strand of wire was a shiny new sign done in reflective paint, which read;

ABSOLUTELY NO TRESPASSING
VIOLATORS WILL BE SHOT
Stirrup Ranch

Chapter 2

Aggie looked up from her coffee to see Billy coming through the café door. The same thrill was there. The same one she always felt when he came into view.

"You're doing better, Billy. You're only ten minutes late." She smiled to tell him she was glad to see him.

"The way things are going out at the ranch, Aggie, I'm lucky to get to town so's you can see me. Right now, I'm just happy to see you and be able to relax a bit."

He slid into the booth beside her. "How've you been, Aggie? I've missed you." He kissed her.

"That's the greeting I've been waiting for," she purred, snuggling under his arm. "Tell me about you, Billy. We can talk about other things after you've relaxed."

#

Arthur "Artie" Newcomb loved to fly. There was no place in Artie's mind for the idea of not flying. Of course, kicking the rudder pedals on a 1956 Piper Tri-Pacer wasn't exactly the same as putting a Phantom through its paces over Nam, but it beat walking.

Artie matched the rudder slant with the wheel and laid the 'Pacer over on its side in a turn as the glint of sunlight off a big reflector caught his eye. He was paid to fly and check out everything. He'd fly for nothing, but since they were paying him, he'd check out everything including the reflection.

Lining the hub of the prop up with the reflection, he reached for the radio mike.

#

Tonio sat in the shade of the big Juniper tree trying to figure out how to make his pay check for the week cover all the bills. Before he'd landed this riding job on Stirrup, he'd been out of work for seven months. He had borrowed from everyone just to eat and keep a roof over Mama and the little sisters. Since his father died, it had all fallen on his shoulders and nineteen year old shoulders aren't used to that kind of a load.

His glance absent-mindedly followed the reins from his hand to the mouth of the hammer headed bay horse attached. The gelding bit off another mouthful of the tall gamma grass, lifted his head, looked at the far horizon, and began chewing.

“Horse, maybe I take that night job and make some real money like Cousin Mariano. But, then again, where can one get paid for laying under a tree most of the day?”

The radio in the saddle bag buzzed just before Artie's message came across, “Stirrup Air One calling any ground unit in the vicinity of Homestead Well.”

“Horse, the well he talks about is just over that hill, so I guess it is us he calls. So much for the laying in the shade.”

Tonio Alverez reached the radio, keyed it, and said, “Tonio here. We are a half mile from the well.”

#

“Crackers, my boy, I don't think they can do this,” Lary said after seeing the second and fourth wires separated from the posts by insulators. “This fence is hot, so you better stay put here in the truck. You hike your leg on that fence and you'll get a thrill the likes of which you ain't never had before.”

Ronson got out and walked to the fence, looking around. The staples and wire gleamed in the afternoon sun without a sign of rust. The footprints of the builders were still clear in the dirt. All the tracks were on the far side of the new wire.

“Somebody fencing others out or themselves in?” He scratched his chin. “I wonder which.”

The fence didn't answer and neither did the dog.

Heading back to the truck, the glimmering wire caught his attention again. Not the fact that it shined, but the fact that 50 yards down the fence line the shining ended. He walked toward the end of the shine.

Old fence - rusting wire, held by staples loose in posts showing signs of rot where they met the dirt - caused Lary to retrace his steps along the fence. In the opposite direction, thirty yards from the road, behind a clump of Junipers, he found the start of old fence and was not surprised. Looking into the tree he could see the solar powered fence charger with a little green light blinking.

"Somebody's just fenced off the gate section. Stirrup must be having problems with trespassers."

"Si, Señor, that is the problem and you are not going to be a part of it. Comprender?"

Lary spun around at the sound of the voice.

Tonio, on the far side of the fence, sat loosely in the saddle atop the big bay with a lever action rifle pointed in Lary's general direction, not at him, but the threat was there.

"What is this? It must be the "Twilight Zone" and I've traveled back in time to the old west." Lary scratched his chin. "But, there wasn't any barbed wire around here until 1935 or so." He stopped talking and looked down at his hip, more than half expecting to see a gun hanging there.

"I am sorry, Señor, but I will have to ask you to move on back the way you have come. You cannot enter Stirrup from this side."

"Well, young fella, I own that section of land over there. The one with the windmill in the middle of it and a cabin about twenty yards west of the mill. Do you know it?"

"Si. I know it. Everybody knows of the Homestead Well. It is the property of Stirrup Ranch."

"Not since my grandfather homesteaded the place it isn't. I own it and I intend to live there. Stirrup has had my permission to use the well and the graze for a long time, a permission I might just change."

"I know nothing of these things, Señor. You will have to talk to Mr. Handley, the owner, or Billy, the foreman, about these things."

"Can you tell me what is going on here?"

"No. It would not be a right thing to do. You talk in town." Tonio pulled the reins of the horse to the right and rode off thirty yards or so, dismounted, hunkered down to watch, the rifle cradled in his arms.

Lary watched him go and for the first time heard the plane circling overhead. He looked up, back to the dismounted rider, waved to both of them, and got in the truck.

Lary turned the truck around and started for town, and the Sheriff's office.

#

Juan Vasquez was hot, tired, and thirsty. The tired and thirsty caused by the twelve miles he had already walked. Most of the hot was because of the man that caused him to walk and thinking of the miles he still had to walk

"I'll get that sucker," he said over and over in a cadence chant as he walked.

Juan knew it would be after sundown when he reached the pavement and that the highway had very little traffic after sundown. If a car wasn't inclined to stop for him, - "and who's going to stop for a scrawny wetback deputy in rags?" he kept asking himself - he could have 30 more miles to walk before he got to the nearest phone.

#

"Aggie, how come you never married that hardware salesman? I don't remember his name, but the one with the new Caddy every year."

Aggie finished chewing her last bit of pie, looking at Billy all the while. As she swallowed, a cute, schoolgirl smile came to her face as she answered, "He never asked me, Bill. Why do you ask?"

"I don't rightly know," Billy said sliding the last dollop of ice cream in his mouth.

Aggie propped her head in her hand, sat her elbow firmly on the edge of the table, and watched him worrying the ice cream to nothing with his tongue. He worked hard to swallow the melted ice cream, like it wasn't an easy thing to do, more like swallowing was painful.

Running his tongue over his teeth and taking a drink of the water seemed to bother him, also. He started fidgeting in his seat and generally appeared uncomfortable.

Aggie knew the look. “What's on you mind, Bill?” She was the only one to call him Bill, and only did so when she was getting serious and wasn't going to be put off.

Billy sat up, looked her in the eye, and said, “Why didn't you ever marry me, Aggie? I asked you often enough.”

“You surely did, Billy, forty-seven times by my count. The first time I was thirteen and you were fifteen. I said yes to you then, if you'll remember, but our parents wouldn't let us and you finally started seeing that hot tamale of a Ramerez girl. The one married to Mariano Alvarez. You know, the big, fat one.”

“Don't remind me. She was cute then.” He grinned. “So, why did you turn me down those other times?”

“You weren't ready, Billy. You just thought you were.”

“Would you marry me now if I asked you?”

“Ask and find out.”

“Will you marry me, Aggie? Right now?”

“No, Bill.” She looked him in the eye, waiting. His entire being fell. She added, “I'm afraid we'll have to wait long enough to get a license and a preacher. A week from now should do it.”

Billy stuck his hand in his pocket, pulled out the makings and rolled a smoke. He looked like he'd lost his best friend, hound dog, and horse, all in the same day. “You mind if I smoke, Aggie?”

“I never have before, Billy. Go ahead.”

He touched a wooden match with his thumb nail, dabbed the flame to the cigarette, and sputtered tobacco, paper, and match all over the table as Aggie's words finally sank in. “You will - a week - preacher. Oh, hell. Aggie, let's go celebrate.”

He kissed her, lifting her bodily out of the booth, spilling the table, plates and all, across the floor and danced her around the café. “By the way,” he shouted, “I love you.”

Aggie threw back her head and said, “By the way, I love you, too.” She was giggling like a school girl of thirteen.

Maria waited until Billy put Aggie down and then said, “If you two ain't gettin' married, you've got a grand bill for busted dishes.”

Billy was grinning from ear to ear and back again, as he said, “She said yes.”

“I figured as much. Congratulations, the crockery's on me. So's the lunch.”

Aggie was being towed toward the door as she said, “Thanks, Maria, you'll get an invite, but right now I think Billy has other things on his mind.”

As the couple danced through the doors, Maria cried, “Don't forget I cater weddings,” a note of sorrow echoed through her voice.

#

Lary stomped the clutch pedal and down shifted through another patch of loose sand. He was mad and taking it out on the old Chevy. Crackers was rolled up, feigning sleep on the floor board. He knew when to disappear.

“Damned people anyhow. They don't know when they're well off. Stirrup didn't have to fence me out. Now, I got half a mind to fence off the well and let them dig their own. What ya think, Crackers?”

The dog opened one eye, thumped his tail just once, and went back to faking sleep.

Lary mashed the clutch against the floor, jammed the stick into third, popped the clutch, and hit the gas. The old truck put forth its best effort, gathering speed in earnest. As the truck rounded a juniper tree, the tattered deputy burst into view directly in the truck's path.

#

Juan's mind was a million miles away trying to wipe out the pain pulsing through his legs and feet. The sound of an engine screamed through his personal discussion causing him to glance back over his shoulder just in time to see a rusting, mostly green truck of questionable vintage careening toward him through the soft sand of the road. From the sight and sound, he was in the wrong place.

Juan might have been tired and whipped to a frazzle, but he was young and had the reflexes of the young. He leaped aside as the truck worked itself to a stop over the spot he had just vacated.

"Sorry about that," came a voice from the cab as the door of the truck opened. "You all right?"

"I'm okay. I was so tired, I wasn't paying any attention and I was walking in the roadway - if you want to call it that." Juan picked himself up and began dusting himself off with his tattered hat.

"My name's Ronson, Lary Ronson. I own Homestead Well." Lary said, sticking out his hand.

"Juan Vasquez here, of late a Deputy Sheriff. I could sure use a ride into town, if you're goin' that way."

"You lose your horse, Deputy?"

"More like had it shot out from under me, I guess you'd say," returning the smile on Lary's face as he answered.

"Hop in. No problem."

#

Chester, "Chet-to-my-friends", Handley waited until all his guests were in the den before saying, "Step up to the bar and tell the man what you'd like. You've all earned a drink."

The four men and two women moved to the bar. Having just returned from a two hour ride through the breaks behind the main ranch buildings, their strides ranged from relaxed to pure pained, and all of them were thirsty.

The man behind the bar was impressive, just like everything at Stirrup headquarters. Shoulders two axe handles wide spread from the base of a neck inside a size 20 collar. The rest of him was a match. His torso was covered with a red blazer adorned with silver conchas and on the breast pocket in gold thread was the Stirrup brand. The blazer covered the Browning Hi-Power under his left arm and the .357 behind his belt at the small of his back. His name was John; it said so over the brand.

John silently handed Mr. Handley a high-ball glass filled with amber liquid before filling the orders of his guests. Anybody watching him closely would notice that John filled the orders deftly, with no wasted motions, and never once did his eyes stop roaming around the room. He saw everything and said little.

Nobody was watching.

Chet hated entertaining these people and was working on never having to do it again. They knew nothing of ranching, never rode unless they were here, and could chatter for hours about the most inane subjects. But, they represented a large voting block of his stockholders. He might still own 51% of the stock, but it was nice to have the other big money on his side. He entertained.

Miss Alicia Mattingly came at him again. She saw a man that was 38, but looked 30. His trim, in-shape body helped carry out the charade of working rancher. His six foot two body was habitually topped with a gray western hat. He looked like a long, lean, lanky cowboy out of a B grade western of the 40's. The image was maintained by all his clothes down to his $1,800 lizard boots and sculpted silver spurs. What Alicia didn't know was that the last time he'd touched a cow was the day his father was killed. He, in turn, had killed that cow.

He saw her coming and said, "Now that you've all got something to refresh yourselves," he sipped his sugar free Ginger Ale, "and before we go into dinner, pull up a chair and we'll talk about the future of Stirrup." Handley waved them all to seats.

The only thing more important to Alicia than a man was money. She sat.

"Thank you, John."

John nodded and left the room. The watchers, if there had been any, would have been surprised to notice his height was only 5' 10". He appeared so much taller behind the bar. But, folks like these didn't watch servants.

#

"If you will please talk one at a time I might be able to figure out what's goin' on," said the Sheriff, swinging his boots to the floor.

Ronson and the Deputy caught their breaths and started again.

"Stop!" The Sheriff stood up. "Juan, you go write your report and get in a clean uniform. Report back here in an hour."

"But, Sheriff . . ."

"Move out."

Juan slammed his tattered hat on his head causing the dust to fly and hang in the air after he stomped out of the office.

"Have a chair, please, Mr. . .?"

"Ronson, Lary Ronson. I own the Homestead Well section and Stirrup has fenced me off. They have denied me access to my property which I want to get to, now.

"I was met at what used to be a gate by a man with a rifle and told I could not go to my property. I want you to do something."

Ben was trying to figure if this was the man the Governor had been promising. He thought, "What a prime man for the job, owning land inside Stirrup and looking like a city boy who has lost his way."

He grinned as he said to Ronson, "Take that seat I offered, Mr. Ronson, and calm down. I'm sure if you had just tried to contact Chet Handley you would have been on your place by now. I'm sure we can get this settled quickly with a phone call."

#

"Crap! Write me a report is all that old man can say. Get on a clean uniform, not - are you okay? - or - what the hell happened to you? - or - nothing. Just write me a report and come back. You'd think that citizen was more important than me and the car getting shot to doll rags."

Juan kept grumbling the whole time it took him to shower, change, and write the report.

He labored over each and every word on that report form, well aware of the Sheriff's temper. He wanted the report to be the best he'd ever done and not one that would add coals to the fire Beazley was going to fan up when he heard his story. Looking at the clock, he realized his hour was up, ten minutes ago.

"And now I'm late to boot. Crap!" He grabbed the papers and headed for the inquisition, mumbling prayers for his probationary career.

#

Two men rode in darkness, seated on the scarred wooden bed of the closed truck. The motorcycles lashed to the sides added a scent of gasoline and hot motor oil to the overpowering smell of cow manure.

"We'll have to get this box vented if I'm going to ride back here again," said the first man.

"Si. I, too, have trouble living and breathing in this stink," answered the second.

They both braced as the truck leaned into a turn onto a dirt road. The first asked, "Whose place we hitting tonight?"

"Quien sabe. It will be a small place or we would have the big truck."

"Mayhaps we'll double up tonight."

"Never have we done so before. I do not think so."

The truck lurched and thumped over a cattle guard, rolled another hundred yards, stopped, and backed to a loading chute. The driver got out, adjusted the hood over his head, and opened the back door of the truck.

The cycles fired and came roaring down the chute with their masked riders stopping at the corral gate to await its opening.

The truck driver opened the gate saying, "Twenty head of the best, por favor. They should be over that rise, there," he swung his arm to the west.

The riders nodded and roared off.

#

Oscar Billings had been a Deputy Sheriff in Apache County for twenty-seven years. Twenty-five of those years, he'd covered exactly the same countryside. He knew all the people, tricks, tracks, and trails of his terrain.

His shift had started at eight that morning and would go until eight the next morning. After that the next two days would be his and he was going fishing with his two nephews.

The sun was down and it was fully dark when Oscar finished his evening meal and coffee at the small diner in the town of Concho.

He paid his bill, used the john, fired up the blue patrol car and rolled west for Snowflake.

The first thing Deputy Billings had done when he started his shift, was to stop at every dirt road and check the tracks. Anything unusual he would check out immediately, otherwise it was just cruise where his nose led him. Throughout his shift, he would slow as he passed each turnoff and check the tracks.

Six miles and fourteen side roads after leaving Concho, he found fresh tracks at the cutoff to the Lazy 7 ranch. His mental alarm was set off by a set of big truck tracks, he knew old man Simonson didn't have a tandem wheeled truck on the place. Lazy 7 just wasn't big enough to cover the expense or have the need of one. Oscar grabbed the mike and tried to raise the office in St. Johns, only twenty miles away.

He got no reply.

Getting no reply didn't surprise him a bit. Apache County was not covered by the best of radio systems. There were dead spots all over the county where you couldn't talk to your next door neighbor on a radio and there wasn't a mountain or building high enough to put a repeater on to cover the whole area. "Someday maybe they'd get a satellite system," he thought.

Counting on trying again a mile or so down the road, the Deputy started following the tracks toward the Lazy 7 headquarters.

The sound of a low-flying plane made him forget all about the radio. Having covered this ground many times before, he knew there was a graded landing strip up ahead about two miles. The strip was the legacy of a long defunct land development's short life. A few abandoned shacks and mobile homes were the only other signs of what had once been lauded as the next Sun City of Arizona.

The tracks took the turnoff to the landing strip.

Oscar followed with his lights out. The setting sun provided just enough light for him to find the shadow of a clump of Junipers to park the car in. Grabbing the pump shotgun from the rack, he started hoofing it toward the sound of idling engines. After a few steps he pumped a round in the chamber.

#

“Sit down. Juan.” The Sheriff Indicated the leather covered recliner in the corner. “Would you smoke a cigar if I gave it to you?”

“I would smoke mule manure right now if I thought it would please you.” Juan figured being totally honest at a time like this was the only way to go.

The Sheriff laughed and handed Juan one of his special cigars from the top desk drawer and said, “Let me read the report while you try to relax. Sit." His years as an Arizona Highway Patrolman before coming to Apache County had given impetus to Ben's voice.

Juan sat.

Taking a wooden kitchen match from a porcelain cowboy boot on the Sheriff's desk, he lit the cigar. For the first time, he noticed that the man he had always looked up to was beginning to gray and his belly stuck out more under his badge. The face was covered with worry lines and the bags under his eyes were beginning to darken. Then Juan remembered that the last birthday the Sheriff had celebrated was his fifty-fifth.

The cigar was a good one, and would have done a lot to calm his nerves if Juan had remembered to smoke it. His anxiety made him forget to draw on the tobacco and, when he finally remembered, he had to reach for another match. The Sheriff read on, apparently concentrating on every word Juan had put on the paper. Just when the Deputy was beginning to relax and enjoy the softness of the chair and the calming effect of the cigar, Beazley said, “Any ideas on who did the shooting? Off the record?”

“Boss, it could have been anybody. I couldn't see much with my face buried in the sand like an ostrich. I will say whoever it was really knows how to shoot. I'll get that sucker for you, Ben.”

“Forget vengeance, he's just another case to bust.

“Now, think hard before you answer this one, Juan. Looking back on the whole thing, is there anything you would do different if the opportunity to do it all over again came along?”

Juan started to speak, but instead laid his head back in the chair, raised his eyes to the ceiling and drew deeply on the unlit cigar in his hand.

Ben grabbed a cigar from the open drawer, licked it and bit the end off. He stared at it for a moment, stuck the stogy in his mouth and wiped a match on the underside of the desk top. "Think on it, Juan. Be sure when you answer." He touched the match to the end of Juan's cigar and then his own, and puffed away. Ben watched the look of total concentration come over Juan's face as the young man went through the whole incident in his mind.

Two years ago, when Ben had first suggested joining the force to Juan, Juan had not been mature enough to think about his own actions like he was doing now. He had been only a wild youngster, walking the thin line between rowdy fun and serious trouble. Ben was totally pleased with this young man and wished there was some way of getting closer to him, like father to son, without seeming to push. Ben smiled.

Five minutes passed as the two men puffed away, filling the room with blue smoke. Juan got out of the chair and walked to the window. It was so dark outside there was no way he could see anything, but he stared into the darkness and continued smoking.

Beazley was lifting his boots to the desk top when the Deputy spun around and said, "No! Damn it, no! There ain't a thing I coulda done different or woulda done different." He flopped in the chair, kicked a leg over an arm and lay back, smoking away with a grin on his face.

"Good. Let's go have a beer. You're buying."

"You're on."

#

Maria Trafoya flipped off the café lights, locked the door, and turned on the alarm. Once again , the stupidity of the alarm hit her. It had cost her a pretty pile of pennies, just to satisfy the insurance company. Diagonally across the intersection was the City Hall and Police station. What more protection could a lady ask for?

She thought of Chet, as she started walking, wondering if he would get rid of his guests and come into town. Chet was the only man in her life and had been since high school, just thinking about his hands caressing her, caused a warm glow to grow from her center and radiate over her entire body.

She entered her house and felt the emptiness of it, an emptiness that wiped out the warmth of her dreams. It wasn't so bad when she had the son home, but now he had his own place and the father didn't come as often because of the building of the ranch.

"Someday he will have time for a wife and son." she said, closing the door. "Someday."

#

"She hurts. She cries. Do not worry, he will be sorry. I promise," a voice whispered to the darkness.

#

Chet Handley watched the last of his guests drive off and chuckled to himself. He'd won every point put forth tonight, without a fight. They were going to back him on the new breeding program, the increased security, and the other improvements he wanted. If things kept going the way they were, he'd soon be the richest rancher in the state since the turn of the century.

He went back to the house, turned off the outside lights and went to the bar. Opening the small refrigerator below the bar, he pulled out a bottle of carrot juice and filled a glass. He got the glass to his lips as John came into the room, dressed in loose white canvas held together with a black canvas belt decorated with red Chinese characters.

"It's that time, is it?" Chet asked, thinking of a more pleasant way to kill the evening.

John nodded.

#

Lary slept fitfully. He hated motels and this bed was the worst bed in the only motel in St. Johns, the Riverside.

Ronson and Sheriff Beazley had talked for twenty minutes before a call had been made to Chet Handley. Ben was told to put the man up at the Riverside, on Stirrup of course, and he, Handley, would come into town in the morning to get this mess all straightened out. Lary had Ben tell the rancher that if he wasn't in town by noon, he would go back the way he'd tried today and make a gate where one was needed.

Lary rolled over, searching for a comfortable, at least less uncomfortable, position.

#

Lenny's was the swingingest joint for a hundred miles around that night. Billy and Aggie were celebrating with the help of the whole drinking population. Juan was drowning his fear and washing the taste of it from his mouth. The Sheriff was helping the couple celebrate and trying to forget the troubles of his office and his life.

Nobody noticed Mariano come in until he sat next to Juan and slapped the Deputy on the back.

"Como esta?" said the Deputy.

"Bien. Y tu?" Mariano replied.

The pair sat and watched the crowd. Mariano ordered a drink from Lenny's new waitress as she strutted by, hips swinging and eyes teasing. "That one will not last long in Lenny's, I think," said Mariano.

"No. She flirts and does not work."

"How goes the war, compañero?"

Juan went into the day and the shooting, and then asked his cousin how things were with him.

"Not well, Juan. Work is hard to find and I may have to go on the road to find it. I will not like to leave, but one cannot live on odd jobs."

Juan shrugged at Mariano as he put a twenty on the table. "Odd jobs pay better than I remember."

"Some do. Some don't," Alverez took his drink and started roving. "The ladies they call, adios," he threw back over his shoulder.

"Or the questions have no answers, my cousin. Someday I will have to stop you, I think," Juan said to his drink, "and my Mother's sister will cry for both of us."

#

Shots sounded in the brush causing the pilot to yell, "Get that stuff out of my airplane if you want it, I'm rolling." He revved the port engine and started the turn that would line the plane up with the open runway, as the man in back carelessly kicked the burlap wrapped bales out of the open door.

When the dirt strip lined off the nose of the plane the pilot looked back and saw that the two tons of cargo were gone. "Get out and close the door or just close the door, I'm taking off now." He revved both engines and checked his gauges. The 'Door closed and locked' light came on. He released the brakes and let the props pull him into the sky.

Chapter 3

Ben awoke with a feeling that said. "Stay in bed, it is going to be one of those days. A cold shower followed by an Alka-Seltzer breakfast didn't do a thing to alleviate the feeling.

Climbing into the beige LTD with the three antennas on the trunk, he said to himself. "Maybe I'm too old for this job and the partying. I'll have to think on which one to give up and which one to keep. Trying to do both is stretching me painfully thin, with an emphasis on the painful." The engine of the car caught on the first try, the noise bringing tears to Ben's eyes.

#

Lary finally gave up on the bed and swore to sleep on the ground before he put another night in that place. Going to the truck, he let Crackers out. "I don't know about your night, fella, but I'll bet you slept better out here than I did in there. Maybe this place should open the rooms to the pets and make the owners sleep in their cars instead of vicey-vercy."

The dog watered three telephone poles, five rose bushes, and all the tires on the truck and the car next to it, before getting back in the cab. Lary opened a can of dog food with the GI P38 can opener on his key ring and filled the dog's dish while the dog washed his face.

Adding water to the other dish he said, "I'll be right back. I'm going to get my own breakfast." He closed the door after cranking the window down and added as he turned away, "Don't let anybody steal the truck."

#

Diane Bennington looked at the clock above the printer. Three hours to go. “This being a dispatcher pays well enough for the amount of work you have to do,” she thought, “but it sure doesn't carry the time by.” She poured another cup of tea from her thermos, added sugar and leaned back with the crossword puzzle covered clipboard on her thighs.

“Now I know why they call this shift the graveyard shift. All the drinkers are in bed by 2 AM and none of the troublemakers are up before noon,” she thought. “If it wasn't for the crossword puzzles, I’d have nothing to do.”

She was just finishing both the tea and the puzzle when the outside door buzzer went off in her ear. She keyed the intercom and said, “Sheriff's Office, may I help you?” as she stood up to look through the window.

“You can help me, but I doubt if anyone can help Billings. He”s dead.”

Diane froze.

“You goin' to let me in, lady, or do I have to stand out here until the funeral?”

The acid in the words got through the numbness in her brain. She started functioning again. She recognized the man at the door as Old Man Simonson, owner of the Lazy 7 Ranch. He was a supposedly harmless old coot and having only had people point him out on the street, she had to go on what she heard. She pushed the button that unlocked the outside door and also told the jailer she was letting someone in.

#

Being a jailer when there wasn't anybody behind the bars was the kind of a job Deacon Washburn liked. Not that he was lazy, it was just that he'd seen all the late, late shows where the jailers get killed, maimed, or otherwise put upon by the inmates at least once a week. The fact that he was black and most of his guests were drunk, redneck cowboys, added some to the unpleasantness of the job. With nobody behind the bars, he could do his clean up chores, the book work, and get a couple of lessons done on his correspondence course. Deac was going to be a computer programmer someday.

He was trying his best to remember the assembly language codes he needed to complete a lesson when the buzzer sounded. The rules said, at the buzzer he had to go to the cross-hatched, iron strapping door between his jail and Diane's office, carrying the shotgun.

He kicked back his chair from the desk, grabbed the empty shotgun, and stood to the door just as Simonson rounded the corner into the hall between his door and her office.

Simonson stopped at the half-door counter to Diane's cubby hole and waited for her to speak.

Diane stood there staring at the visitor.

Deacon got worried, so worried he broke the rules. He opened the iron door, walked to the door and said, “What's the matter?”

She didn't answer him, the old man did, “I just found Billings shot to doll rags out by that landing strip near my place. She must be new here and never heard of a dead man before.”

Washburn reached over the counter, opened the half-door, and went in. Standing the shotgun against the wall, he grabbed the dispatcher by the shoulders and gently guided her to the chair. He looked back at the old rancher and said, “Billings was her uncle.”

The jailer picked up the mike and said in a voice much calmer than the rest of him, “We have a deputy down at the airstrip on the road to the Lazy Seven. Turn off is," he paused while he checked the map on the wall, “eight tenths of a mile west of mile post 316 on the Concho/Snowflake highway.”

Deacon listened to the rattle of responses and, figuring he'd done a good job, was about to congratulate himself, when Diane said, “The Sheriff didn't respond to the call. Give me the mike, Deac. And, thanks.”

#

Ben was on his second cup of coffee when Lary came through the door, stretching and rubbing his back. Lary looked around the diner. The Sheriff caught his eye and motioned toward the seat opposite him in the booth.

Lary smiled, sat and said. “Good morning."

“Not very. I feel like the 1st Marine Division stomped across my head on their way from the Chicago stock yards. A few of their boots must have hit my mouth, the taste is horrible.”

“I never have figured out why I gave up drinking; whether it was the cost or the feeling of the morning after.”

Lary turned his cup right-side-up as the waitress came by with the coffee pot. He took a long draw at the weak coffee and said. “I’m just not myself in the morning until I've had two cups of coffee. As weak as this is, it'll probably take three or four to get my motor running. I thought all these cowboy cafés had coffee that would float a horseshoe with the horse still attached.”

“Not this one. The only thing they use plenty of in this place is red chili. You're in luck; they don't put chili in the coffee. They do put it in everything else.”

“Good, I like my food spicy. It helps to keep the motor running after the coffee gets it started.”

“I wish I could get my motor to quit running. The noise is killing me.” The Sheriff’s breakfast came as he finished the statement. He put his cup down and looked at the plate of food; much of it had a reddish tint. Lary thought the Sheriff was going to lose his breakfast before he ate it.

“Would you care for some eggs and sausage, Mr. Ronson?” the sick man asked, pushing his plate across the table.

“I'd love some. Thank you, Sheriff.” Lary grabbed the silver and shoved the first bite in his mouth. “Are you sure you don't want any, Sheriff.”

Ben got up and lurched for the door marked “Pointers” for an answer.

#

“Will you need me at the café today, Mamacita?”

“No, Miquelito, thank you. You have fun on such a beautiful day.” She dug in her purse and came out with a twenty. “For you. Impress a girl, my son.”

“Gracias, Mama. I will try!”

#

Juan didn't have a car, so he walked up to the courthouse and went in the door marked “County Sheriff.” Diane was standing with her back to the door. Old Man Simonson was sitting on the bench across the hall with a cup of coffee in his hand. The old man looked up as Juan stepped through the door, slowly shook his head, and went back to drinking from the white mug.

Deacon Washburn was standing in front of the old man. He, too, had a steaming cup in his hand. Deacon took one look at the new arrival and breathed an audible sigh of relief.

Diane looked around at the sound.

“Am I glad to see you, Juan.” the black man started, “All hell's busted loose and there ain't a fire hose in this here county that'll reach it.”

Simonson mumbled something under his breathe about the combined intelligence of a wetback and a nigra.

“If I didn't need you around to give a statement, I'd kick your bigoted backside from here to that run down hole in the range you call a ranch. You make one more crack and I'll lock you up for loitering and take your statement from a cell,” the female dispatcher screamed.

Simonson started to stand and was met by a pair of stiff arms, one brown and one black, that impressed him with their combined persuasiveness.

“Just sit right there and keep your mouth shut until the Sheriff gets here to take your statement,” Deac said through clinched teeth.

Deacon added. “One more move out of you, until you're called upon, and I'll be more than happy to put you in a nice, freshly cleaned cell.”

All three of the deputies turned their backs on the man.

Diane pulled a fresh cup from the rack and filled it. She handed it to Juan who, seeing the tears on her cheeks, asked, “What gives?”

#

Billy kissed Aggie goodbye, stating, “Another week and I won't get a sore back from that danged couch.”

"We'll just have to come up with something, won't we, Billy?" The twinkle in her eye and smile on her face held promises for the cocky foreman.

Billy doffed his hat with a wide, sweeping motion until his forearm was across his waist and then bowed deeply. "Thank you for the breakfast, madam. As to the hint of further pleasures in your abode, I await breathlessly the fulfillment."

"Sir Walter Raleigh you aren't, but I'll get by somehow."

He slapped his hat back on his head with a flourish. "I'll bet I could teach Sir Walter how not to lose his head and a couple of other tricks, if I tried, Aggie."

"I'll just bet you could, Bill. I'll just bet you could." She paused. "Off with you now or we'll both get fired for not making it to work on time."

She turned to go and he slapped her playfully on the backside.

She grabbed the broom from behind the door and chased him down the walk with it swinging close to his head. He saved himself by jumping into the bed of his pickup truck, which she couldn't do in the form fitting business suit she was wearing.

She tried to reach him with the broom, laughing so hard she had trouble seeing her target for the tears. He jumped to the ground on the far side, got in, and drove off, screaming and shouting, "Help, save me." at the top of his lungs.

Aggie stood at the curb and waved him off with the broom until he rounded the corner and was gone from sight. Waving the broom at the neighbors on both sides, she skipped to the door, singing, "Won't you marry me, Bill?"

After he stopped laughing, Billy reached down and turned on the radio below the dash and set the dial to scan. The first channel checked was the Sheriff's frequency. He slammed on the brakes and his jaw dropped as word of the Deputy's death came through loud and clear. When the main message ended it was followed by a call for the Sheriff which didn't get answered.

Across the intersection from where he had stopped was the El Charro café and in the parking lot was Ben's LTD.

#

Ben Beazley stormed the office like the Marines up Mount Sirabachi. The first thing he saw was Deac and Juan in front of the Dispatch Office glaring at Old Man Simonson.

"What's this about Billings being shot up?" he yelled.

Everybody started talking.

#

Lewellen Garth was the first deputy to arrive at the airstrip. As Simonson had said, the man was shot to shreds. At least five large caliber holes could be seen and no less than three charges of shot had hit the body. One shotgun blast had been done at close range directly into Oscar's face. Never a good looking man, Billings was not a sight for weak stomachs as he lay twisted in death.

He got out the ribbon. Cordoning off the area was the first thing he did before working out the tracks. Being the court recognized expert tracker for the Sheriff's Department didn't allow him too much slack. He had to be careful. The body in the area was a friend's and that made him even more concerned. Knowing that DPS would probably be called in on a Deputy down made him think on every move he made. He didn't want to screw up the evidence that might catch the man or men who did this to his friend and mentor.

The ribbon strung and camera around his neck, he stepped into the area. Six clicks of the camera passed before he reached Oscar's body. The camera clicked through a roll of film as Lew walked slowly around the body at a distance of ten feet. He was sure of the distance. There was a string clipped to Billings belt that was attached to the camera. The string was exactly ten feet long.

The sound of engines screaming and tires crunching sand made Lew head for his car.

Two more Deputy Sheriffs had arrived.

Bud Martin got out of his LTD and eased in behind Shef Petty, as the second deputy ran for the twine. Shef met Lew's stiff arm and stern face at the twine.

"Ain't no need for you to go in there, Shef. I'll do the inside work, you and Bud get things sorted out outside the string."

"Damn it, Lew. Oscar was my friend and I'm not going to let somebody kill him and get away with it."

"Good. We're agreed on that. I'll be extra careful with the material evidence in here and you do the same out there. Keep an eye on Bud and make sure he goes along with us. You know how he likes to let things slip by all the time."

The last caught Shef up short. Bud had never let anything slip by him at any time. In fact, when the Sheriff had an extra tough one, he called Bud.

Shef might be a hot head, but he was nobody's dummy. When he set his mind to running there weren't too many things that slipped by. He calmed down and walked back to the car for his camera and clip board. Bud did the same, nodding to Lew with a smile which said. "You done good," to the younger man.

Bud and Shef talked for a couple of minutes and then went to work in opposite directions around the cordoned off area. Lew turned his attention to the inside.

They hadn't taken ten steps when the outside speakers on all three vehicles started screaming with Beazley's voice. Ben wasn't fooling, they could tell by the fact he was talking plain English and not all the mumbo-jumbo that usually crossed those airwaves.

#

The Sheriff waited with the mike in his hand until somebody at the airstrip answered.

It was Bud.

"Bud, I want you to take charge of the scene. Keep Lew and Shef with you. Champ is on his way. Use him to control the site and keep the sightseers out of the way. All the rest of the boys will continue on the day's calls."

"I'm in charge. Lew and Shef work on the case with me. Champ for traffic control. Is that it, Ben?"

"For now. Out!" Bud sat the mike on the radio and started giving orders in a calm, relaxed voice. This is what he lived for, THE case.

"Diane - Get the governor's office on the phone. After them, I want to talk to Department of Public Safety Director Woods.

Juan - You take Mr. Simonson into the briefing room and get his statement. Don't forget to thank the man for the time he has given and will give to help us in this case. Remember, without concerned citizens like Mr. Simonson, our job would be a lot harder."

"Deac - You got anybody back there?" stabbing a finger at the cell block.

"No, Sir! Nary a soul."

"Good. Take over on the radio. Cut in the speaker in my office and put on a new tape. I don't want to miss anything. You aren't a certified Deputy, so I'll ask you to play secretary/dispatcher for a spell, if you don't mind."

"Will do," Deac added under his breath, "beats heck out of scrubbln' toilets and changing puked on beds."

Everyone was still standing where Ben had found them when he walked in, so he added. "Move!" somewhat less than calmly. All traces of a hangover were gone. His fourteen years as Sheriff coming to the surface overshadowing all signs of the morning after. He walked to his office with a swagger not seen in years.

Old Man Simonson followed Juan, mumbling under his breath about how it was time somebody around here realized that it was men like him who not only elected, but paid the salaries of the Sheriff and his motley crew. He was glad the Sheriff understood that. "But, being a white man, he would," he mumbled.

#

Lary Ronson finished his breakfast and tried to pay the bill. Maria informed him that Stirrup was covering it and asked him if he would like something for the dog.

"How did you know I had a dog with me, ma'am?"

"If you stay long in this town, Mr. Ronson, you'll find that there are not many secrets. We are a small group of people, many related by blood, marriage, or both. And, secrets just do not stay secret very long. It has been said of our town, that others know when a girl is pregnant before she does."

"I'll keep that in mind. Thanks for the meal, it was great."

"I am glad it was not too hot for you. I had fixed it for the Sheriff, to help fix up his hangover and added a few things to help him out."

"Nothing deadly, I hope."

"No." she laughed, "Only chilies and some herbs to help clean out his system."

He laughed in return and made for the door. "I'll be back," he said over his shoulder.

#

Chet Handley was sore, really sore. A careful exam during his shower showed bruises on his side and a lump on his shoulder. "I'll have to do more practicing on how to fall." He chuckled.

John had worked him over the night before. The only break was when the Sheriff called about the dude from Homestead Well. One of these days he was going to be showing John how to fall. That would be an interesting day.

His preoccupation with the stockholders meeting had cost him the bump and bruises. That was over and done with, and now it was time to go meet this Ronson and make him happy. Maybe he should have spent the night with Maria. He might still be sore, but it would be a better feeling sore.

Chet hit the switch on the intercom next to his dresser and waited.

"Yes, sir," came the voice from the box.

"John, it's time to get into town and settle this matter of Homestead Well with Ronson. Meet me at the car in ten minutes. Bring my breakfast with you."

"Ten minutes. Yes, sir."

"Tell dispatch to expect vehicles moving toward Homestead later this morning. Ours will be one of them."

"Yes, sir."

Chet dressed in subtly faded and worn Levis, a blue denim western cut shirt, and pulled on his elephant hide work boots. He debated on which spurs to wear before deciding that spurs were a nuisance in the car. He went out in bare boots.

Near the front door, he stopped in front of a full length mirror, added wallet, gold pen and the old beat up hat, and checked his image in the mirror again. He frowned, cocked the hat a little more to the right, grinned, nodded, and went out the door.

#

Beazley called Deac into his office after completing his calls. “Where do we stand?”

Deac consulted a spiral notebook after pulling it from his shirt pocket, “Bud has things under control at the site. Lew says there are more tracks out there than he can keep track of. He makes it eight men, a pickup, a heavy tandem six-wheeled truck, and a plane - twin engine. The ambulance is still in route, but Dr. Peters has been and gone. He confirmed Lew's findings. Oscar is dead. Lew has the boys plaster casting and photographing everything twice and some items three times.

“For other evidence, they have five shotgun hulls and twelve cases of the following calibers,” he checked his notes, “Five .38 special, three .45 Colt Auto, and four .30 caliber carbine. Lew says one of the shotgun hulls is from Oscar's riot gun. There are a couple of drops of blood forty-five feet away from Oscar's body, indicating the possibility one of the assailants was hit."

“I don't suppose you've put the word out to the hospitals and doctors to be on the lookout for a wounded man. They may not recognize a wound from a couple of pellets to be a gunshot wound unless they’re on the lookout,” Ben said quietly.

“I did that as soon as we got the word.”

“Good.”

“Anything more I can do?”

Ben checked his watch. “No, Deac. I think it’s time you went home and got some sleep. It's after nine and you were supposed to be off shift at eight. You know I'm not authorized to pay overtime and there just aren't enough people on the staff to make comp-time work.” He picked his cigar out of the ash tray and struck a match to it. “You've done a fine job today. I’ll try to make this up to you. Thanks.”

"It keeps gettin' exciting around here and I may just opt to be a Deputy instead of a programmer."

"Programming must pay better and has to be more regular in hours."

"Money ain't everything and I've never worked a job with regular hours. I think I'd have trouble adapting to a routine, dull, rut of a job. This is going to call for some thinking." The black man scratched his head, smiled, and added. "You ain't planning one of them computerized cars - like the one on the tube - in the near future are you, boss?"

"I have trouble getting cars with a pair of lights on top from the Supervisors, how in the name of Hades do you think I could convince them I need, underline need, a computerized car."

"Would you like me to try it for you?" he said, his face split by a toothy smile.

"Go home. You're so tired, you're getting silly. If there's anything I don't need today it's a case of the sillies."

"Goodnight, boss."

"Goodday, Deac. Leave the door open and tell whoever replaced Diane to kill the speaker in here. Make sure Diane went home, too, will ya, Deac?"

"She left, and I'll get Lane to kill the speaker." He turned and walked slowly out of the office. His body noticeably slumping at each step. The last view the Sheriff had of him as he turned into the hall Deac was wiping his face with a palm and shaking his head.

"It's already been a long day," Ben said quietly to the retreating back.

Ben reached for the phone to call the Department of Public Safety to bring them in on the investigation as the law requires when an officer is downed. Made sense that you didn't want the team that he worked for investigating the shooting, they just might be a bit prejudiced.

#

"You must be Mr. Ronson. I'm Chet Handley of Stirrup Ranch." He extended his hand.

"I won't ask how you knew, but I can guess. I was the only stranger in the place. Right?"

"Right."

Lary took the offered hand and felt the pressure of the handshake. "This guy is stronger than he looks," Lary thought.

Chet thought, "This guy has done more than just ride a desk," as he felt the returned pressure.

The two men grinned at each other with a look which said, 'We're pretty well matched in this, we'll have to find another way to compete.'

"Mr. Ronson," Chet started, dropping the hand, "I sure am sorry about this mix up. If you had written or called, and let me know you were coming, I would have made arrangements for you to have access to your property. You have been very fair and honest in your dealings with Stirrup and I would in no way want to jeopardize those dealings. It would be too expensive for Stirrup."

"The move was kind of sudden and I really wanted to have a little peace and quiet before anybody found out I was there," Lary said with more than a hint of mystery in his voice. "What in the world is going on around that place that makes you do away with gates and station armed riders and patrolling aircraft on the place. Oh, yeah, and electrified fences."

"It's a long story. Why don't I ride with you and we can talk about it, and our future dealings on the way to the ranch."

"Fair enough."

"Would you do me the honor of staying at Stirrup while you are getting the cabin at Homestead Well ready to live in?" Chet's smile was as warm as that of a used car salesman.

"I'd be happy to and I'll take it as an honor to stay with you." Lary's voice held just a hint of sarcasm. "Right this way to the Ronson limo. By the way, you'll have to share the seat with my dog. You don't mind dogs, do you?"

"Not really."

#

Maria watched Chet leave with the stranger and was almost overwhelmed by the hurt. He hadn't even looked at her. He hadn't even been kind enough to acknowledge her existence. Maybe, it will all be right when the ranch was set up and he has time for a wife and son. At least, that is what he had been telling her for all these years.

She should be used to it by now, she thought as she returned to the kitchen.

#

“Thank you, Mr. Simonson, and we'll be in touch if there's anything more we need from you concerning this matter. You have been most cooperative.” Juan held the door open for the old man.

“Glad you finally realized who butters your bread, youngster," Simonson said, ducking through the door, quickly.

Juan let the door close, mumbling a few choice words under his breath. He'd done everything the Sheriff had asked and had done it with a smile. It wasn't the prettiest smile he’d ever worn, but a smile nevertheless.

It was a waste. The old man hadn't seen anything that was going to help the investigation. All he'd done was find the body and he hadn't even gone near enough to make sure Oscar Billings was really dead. He'd called a couple of times and, when the man didn't answer, assumed the deputy was dead. The old coot had gone back to his house, eaten breakfast, and then came into town to report the shooting.

Deputy Vasquez took the statement into the Sheriff.

#

The explosion came exactly two minutes and eighteen seconds after Ben started reading Simonson's statement.

“He did what? Had breakfast. Didn't check him out. That damned old sour faced son of a sheep castrator had better never come into this office looking for a favor. I'd rather help forty-seven wetbacks get jobs than. . .”

Juan quit watching the clock and closed the door to Ben's office the rest of the way, the sound of the tirade fading with the closing of the door.

#

“Today is the beginning of the end for Stirrup,” the mind behind the 7mm Magnum said.

#

Crackers lay on the floor boards looking up at the stranger in his seat. Lary knew from the dog's actions that he didn't like this man. Why? He didn't have the foggiest idea, but Crackers wasn't having anything to do with this intruder.

“Maybe the dog has the right idea.” he thought.

Lary's first opinion, which wasn't necessarily the one he was going to end up with, was that this man had blown his own importance all out of proportion to his position in the community. No matter how big the ranch, it didn't employ enough or pay enough taxes to warrant the big headedness Handley exhibited. Lary also wondered why he felt so ill at ease in the man's presence.

“You know, Ronson, this ranch has a ways to go yet, but it's going to be the finest in the southwest one of these days. You could be a part of it. I'll swap you for Homestead Well. Stock in Stirrup is at a high of sixteen-twenty right now, but if you want to swap, I'll give you stock at the value it was at the low last month, twelve-seventy a share."

Lary maneuvered the truck around a long slow curve, checking the mirror for John and the Limo. It was there and so was the driver. He got the distinct feeling, Handley was telling him, not asking. He said, “Homestead Well is not for sale.”

Chet absentmindedly reached to pet the dog and was warned off in no uncertain terms. “That dog is dangerous, Ronson. He tried to bite me.”

“If Crackers wanted to bite, you would be bleeding now. I repeat. Homestead Well is not for sale. You don't have enough money to buy the only thing that could be considered an heirloom in my family.”

#

Lew wiped the sweat from his face with a red handkerchief as he surveyed the landing strip area. Oscar’s body was gone. The only reminders that there had ever been a body here were the blood stains in the sand surrounded by red plastic ribbon and a trail of twine from the outer perimeter to the spot.

He said to himself, “I wonder if I'll end up like that, alone in some God forsaken spot, shot to hamburger?”

“Nope, you and me are goin' to live to bounce our great-grandkids on our bony, arthritic knees.” Bud was immediately sorry about the choice of words.

Lew turned to find Bud hunkering down, rolling a smoke. “I've got to get the kids before I'll ever have something to bounce on my knees. Sue was at the doctor's again yesterday and he still doesn't hold out a lot of hope for us.” His eyes lowered as he spoke.

“There's always adoption. Matter of fact if I could talk the wife into it, you could have a couple of ours.”

“I wouldn't want to cut into your baseball team. You need all nine of them kids and there ain't no way that wife of yours is going to part with any and neither are you.”

Lew took the makings from Bud as Bud said, “Make that ten. Carrie just brought home the good news last night. Man, someday I'm going to have to find out what's causin' all these kids and put an end to it.”

“As rutty as you are, there'll be younguns around your place until Carrie says whoa biologically. Seems we ought to be able to work out a happy medium between the two of us, instead of you getting them all. Somehow it just don't seem hardly fair.” Lew was smiling outside, but the pain showed through his eyes.

Bud saw the pain and changed the subject. “What do you figure happened here, Lew? Why'd he get caught so easy? Oscar wasn't a rookie.”

“From the tracks, I'd say he walked into it just like a hot headed kid with something to prove to the old timers. If it had been Juan or Shef, I could understand it, but Oscar was cautious, real cautious. Too cautious for my blood, but he had lived for a long time in this business and in this territory. He knew what the sound of an airplane meant out here at that time of night, especially with the cars and trucks thrown in. We been talking about that scenario in meetings for a couple of years now.

"I'd love to be able to wake him up and have him answer two questions for me. One, why did he go in without radioing for help? Two, who did it to him like that?"

"You think we'll find out. Bud?"

"Not likely, unless we get a break. But, this work always counts on a certain amount of luck and breaks. If we don't get those guys on this, you can bet somebody will get them for something. These suckers never stop until they're stopped by the likes of us, or their competition."

Bud looked around, ground out his butt, and said, "What do you figure they were doing, loading or unloading."

"Unloading."

"What?"

"Top quality stuff. One of the bales broke apart over there and this is what was in it." He handed the older man a baggie containing what appeared to be marijuana. "Nothin' but the finest in smokin' for the boys in Apache County."

"You test it, yet?"

"Yep, yellow as yellow can be. Mighty high class stuff. From the marks in the sand, they dropped at least twelve bales of this stuff. I'd say the bales went around fifty kilos each from the dent they made."

"Goin' to be a high time in this old county for a spell. I just can't believe they're going to travel far with that much, Lew."

"There's enough of this stuff to do quite a few comparisons, why don't we try and catch a couple of the users and trace this back up the line."

"I'll run that idea past Ben when we get back. You done here?"

"One more once-over in this new light is all I want. I like to give the sun a couple of hours to change the shadows and go over it again, before I call it done. Shouldn't take me more than another hour. You two don't have to wait on me."

“All right, I'll leave Champ here to control any sightseers that happen to show up. Shef and I will go write this up and tell Ben what's what.”

“Leave the smokes, will ya? I'm out.”

Bud tossed the can of Prince Albert and papers, waved, and headed for Shef who was still working on the perimeter.

Lew shouted, “Thanks.”

Lew turned back to the scene, wondering what he might have missed. His mind was not on the job and he hoped that the extra look-over would make up for his lack of concentration. His thoughts were mostly of Sue and the depression she was in. The doctor was even worried that she might consider herself less than a whole woman due to her inability to have children. Lew wanted to be with her and comfort her, but a crime like this always called for his talents, talents he wished he'd never found.

Chapter 4

Aggie sat behind her desk in the County Recorder's office, smiling. It had been so unexpected, but so wanted. Bill was her only real beau and always had been. Up to now he had been too set on having a good time all by himself. Now he was ready to work in tandem like a good set of mules ahead of a plow. Somehow the analogy pleased her.

Pastor Smalley and the Baptist Chapel were set for the wedding. Flowers would be there, as would Maria to cater. Carrie Martin, her best friend, had agreed to stand with her and help hold her up. Carrie had even offered to give her a couple of kids for a wedding present, but withdrew her offer when Aggie had said she didn't want to break up the team and, "Besides, homegrown is more fun all the way around."

Aggie's phone had been extremely busy, with all her outgoing calls getting the arrangements for the wedding made. And then there were all the incoming office business calls that kept interrupting. All she had left was to get Billy to the license window, and the altar, which based on his history, may not be as easy as it sounds. Cows have always come first with Billy.

Of course, there was the hair dresser and the dressmaker to contend with before the week was done and the ceremony a thing of the past. Invitations were easy, one big poster on the Post Office door. Everybody went to the Post Office.

#

Carrie Martin guided the shopping cart down the aisles of the St. Johns Supermarket, cussing the prices each step of the way. If they kept going up, she and Bud would be getting slimmed down just so the team could eat. Once again she thought philosophically about a religion which said, have all you can and don't use any precautions, it's a sin. “Oh, well, God will provide, always has, always will.”

She saw Sue Garth round the end of the row of shelves and was reminded of the new life inside her own body. There had to be a fairness somewhere for the two of them, she with so many and the younger woman with none. “Why would God provide me with so many and her with none? Is there no balance to His blessings? Am I a better person or something? ”

The hurt shown in the barren woman's eyes as she moved gracelessly down the aisle listlessly looking at this and that, taking up a can and then putting it back without even looking at it. The dress she wore was a shapeless thing with washed out dead colors that she must have bought years ago. Her face was not made up and her hair was carelessly pulled back into a tangled, bedraggled ponytail. No one had to look twice to tell she thought herself a failure as a woman. It was written all over her.

Coming close, Carrie said, “Hi, Sue.”

“Oh,” Sue looked around. “Hi.”

“Is something wrong, you look down in the dumps?”

“Could we talk, Carrie?”

“Anytime. Let's check out and go to your place. You make better tea than I do.”

“I've only got a couple more things to pick up, so you go ahead and I'll be right behind. The front door's unlocked as usual.” She started down the aisle again, mumbling, “I wonder if they have some of that good crumb cake in the bakery? Maybe some éclairs, or how about some donuts. I'll just have to get some.”

Carrie watched her young friend go and the conversation she had with her neighbor last night came fresh to her. Her neighbor was the Doctor's receptionist and the whole story of the younger woman's visit yesterday was told over the back fence. There was nothing that the Doctor could find wrong with Sue. She wanted children so bad that the Doctor felt the problem was one of tension and fear.

Tension from wanting and fear of not getting.

"All I have to fear is running out of food and space with the mob I have. Please, God, make this the last one. Or, keep the miracles coming." She was constantly having a conversation with her God and felt He heard and cared enough to respond.

Something would work out. Carrie was sure of it.

#

The heavily loaded pickup eased through the turnoff onto the road which would lead to Stirrup. Chet was still trying to form some type of a partnership with Larry, with the Homestead Well section taking part as the only blue chip in the game.

"Look, Handley, like I've been trying to tell you, Homestead is going to stay in my name, under my control for the foreseeable future. I will continue to lease the use of the land and the well to Stirrup at a reasonable price.

"Your Dad built the fence around the place and the cattle traps at the well. You have maintained those things and the well for quite a few years without asking me for any help. I don't see why that arrangement shouldn't continue. And, if it will make you feel any better, I'll put all this in writing. A long term contract might be arranged for your benefit. All I want is a refuge."

It was the longest speech either of the two men had made during the entire trip out from town. Crackers thumped his tall once as if he were in agreement with what was just said. Both men fell silent.

Ronson had managed to get the truck up to 45 and into third gear before Chet said, "Fair enough. Let's shake on it and call a truce and talk of other things."

"Done."

Crackers' tail thumped the floor board again.

#

The scope scanned the truck and picked out the figure of Handley sitting in the passenger seat. The eye behind the scope recognized the driver as the stranger from the café. The second car was scanned with equal care and when the eye was sure only John was in the vehicle, the sight shifted to the right front tire.

The finger on the trigger squeezed.

The shoulder felt the kick of the 7mm round.

The tire went flat, instantly.

#

Chet Handley was moving for the floor boards before Larry realized what had happened. Crackers stopped Handley's move for cover cold, with bared teeth and a low growl.

The fact that the sound he had just heard was a gunshot hit Larry Ronson. Hitting the gas, he yelled at the dog and shoved Chet onto the floor with the dog,

“Did they hit John? What about John and the other car? Can you see anything back there, Ronson?” Chet's voice was far from normal.

“The other car is stopped in the middle of the road. No sign of the driver. Looks like a tire on the front might be flat.” Larry replied, calmly.

“The first sound was a shot, Ronson. That was no blowout. The shot must have gotten the tire. John in sight, yet?”

“No sign of him. What do you want to do? There’s a pistol in the glove box if you need it.”

Chet laughed. “That pea shooter against a 7mm Magnum could be the theme for a modern western movie. Let’s just get to Stirrup. It's only another couple of miles and I'll get a couple of the boys to go back with me. Properly armed, of course. You can call the Sheriff while I'm out rounding up the posse.” He paused as he climbed up to the seat, “Maybe, just maybe, this man, whoever he is, has gotten himself in too far this time. We just might be able to get him caught between the Deputy Ben sends out, and me and the boys.”

Larry asked. “Could there be a part in this for me a little bigger than calling the Sheriff and saying, 'They went thataway.'?”

“Can you shoot?”

“Cat got climbing gear? Bear crap in the woods? Snake got hips? Chicken got lips? Gladys Knight sing with the Pips? You bet your booties I can shoot, Marines - Expert.”

"If you were a Marine, we'll take you along."

#

John was hoping for the Marines. Every time he stuck his head up a 7mm round came calling. His short barreled pistols were next to useless and so was his funny looking black belt.

He worked his way across the car to open the door on the side away from the shooter. He found that body metal and windows don't stop 7mm rounds. He crawled under the car, putting as much metal as possible between himself and the end of the barrel on the high powered Magnum, wishing John Wayne hadn't died and was leading the Cavalry to the rescue.

#

Juan was rolling, in the Sheriff's own car. He was going to get the shooter, this time. Juan had taken the call from Ronson. He was nearest to the scene. The Sheriff said. "Sic,em!" tossing Juan the keys.

The needle on the speedometer was buried. The two lane road passed under the radial tires in a blur that made Juan wonder what would happen if one of the tires let go. He slowed up only when he saw the cutoff road to the ranch coming up fast, way too fast.

A controlled, drifting slide carried the LTD and Juan around the cutoff corner and onto another straightaway. A couple of hundred yards up the road, Juan saw the disabled car, aslant in the road. A 7mm hole spiderwebbed the windshield of the LTD and a heavy force hit the back of the front seat within inches of the frantically braking Deputy.

Before the big Ford could come to a stop, Juan had it in reverse and stomped the gas. "You ain't taking this car out. Crap. No, you ain't," he screamed over the scream of tires trying to find purchase on the asphalt.

Juan was ready this time. A rifle lay on the floor boards of the LTD. It wasn't as potent as the 7mm, but .308 wasn't a caliber to be sneezed at. The Remington rifle had a three-to-nine power scope on top and Juan knew this rifle. It was his and, only last week he had sighted it in at 250 yards planning on using it for the upcoming deer season. Now, he was glad it was ready.

The Deputy parked the Sheriff's car behind a cedar tree a good 200 yards from the disabled Stirrup car. Juan tossed his hat in the back seat. His badge went in a shirt pocket. He took to the woods.

The phone call had indicated that the shooter was on the south side of the road. The round through the windshield verified that. How far back off the road hadn't been guessed at. Juan decided he'd try to come up behind the shooter about three hundred yards off the road and work in toward the disabled car. For once he was hoping to hear the sound of the heavy rifle, pointed in the other direction, of course.

#

Billy listened to the radio and was scared. Was his boss okay? Was the stranger? What was going on now that Juan had sent in the message he was out of the car? He put his boot heel on the pedal hoping to get a little more speed out of the truck.

Coming around the turnoff corner, he spotted the Sheriff's car. Sliding the truck to a barely controlled stop, he grabbed the AR-15 from the rack over the back window, a couple of thirty round magazines from the glove compartment and a .45 Colt Peacemaker from under the seat. Jamming a magazine in the rifle, he stepped from the truck just in time to hear the heavy report of the 7mm. He hit the dirt with .45 in one hand and rifle in the other.

It took him awhile to realize the shot was a long way off. Chuckling to himself, he checked the loads in the .45, tucked it in the back of his belt, and started toward the shooter saying. “And Aggie said this wasn't the 1880's. Seems to me she might be a bit wrong on that.”

#

Chet tossed an .30 caliber carbine to Larry and said. “This suit you?”

“No. Got anything that will reach out more than a yard or two?” tossing the carbine back.

"How about an ought-six Springfield? It was my father's and shoots true."

"That'll do. What are you using?"

"An ought-six, Model 70 Winchester to be exact. Let's git, if you're ready."

Larry beat him out the door and into the jeep, which already contained two armed men.

#

"Damn it! Isn't there another deputy in this county that we can get down there to help Juan?" Ben was fuming as the dispatcher tried to find anyone within 30 minutes of the gun fight. With Juan out of the car there was no communication with him and she knew the Sheriff's frustration level was already low and was now going to go through the ceiling.

"They're all on their way. Everyone that can get away from what they were already on. You want a rundown?" answered a cool Lane. She hadn't been a dispatcher for sixteen years to be flustered by this situation. She'd been through worse many times.

"No. I just need something to growl at." He returned to his office cussing because he'd let Juan go alone and because of the way he growled at Lane, again.

#

Juan trotted over the unfamiliar terrain, knowing that he was closing on something he really didn't want to get too close to. The weight of the rifle in his hands and the pistol on his hip were the only reassurance he had. His abilities with both helped him continue to move forward. That, and the thought of redeeming himself in the Sheriff's eyes.

Easing slowly to the top of a hillock, he took a peek through a gap between two thick clumps of blue sage at what was on the other side. "Shoot now you scumbag, shoot now." he whispered.

He moved around slowly, widening his field of view. With agonizing attention to detail, he scanned everything in sight through the scope on the rifle. An ant crawled across his arm. He didn't feel it. Beads of sweat formed in the channel of his spine. He didn't feel that, either. His total concentration was on the dirt and scrub before him.

Nothing was out there that he could find.

Nothing.

"Damn! There's something out there. Something that shoots at things and people," he said to himself and a raven soaring overhead. "But, where?"

He eased the rifle through another gap in the sage and continued the search through the scope.

#

Chet ordered the jeep stopped before they rounded the curve which would have put the disabled car in sight. "You two go around that way and see if you can give John a hand. Try to cover him so he can get out of there. If he's still in there.

"If he's already in the clear, do what he tells you. Don't take any chances, this guy can shoot and I don't want anybody hurt," he said, pointing down one side of the road. Under his breath, he added, "Except that idiot with the big gun up there."

After watching the two hired hands go in the direction Chet pointed, Larry started toward where he thought the shooter would be at a steady lope. Chet followed, listening for the planes he'd ordered into the area.

#

Billy saw the Deputy lying at the top of the next rise and stopped, huffing and puffing like an old steam engine. Once again, he vowed to quit smoking, tomorrow. Cawing like a raven, he tried to attract Juan's attention. Billy stood up and waved his arms. He shouted.

Juan didn't respond. Billy moved on.

#

The grin on Artie's face went from ear to ear. He was back in the air again. The look on his face was one of total contentment with the world and maybe just a little mastery of his own particular world. He never felt this way on the ground. Below him, the road from the highway to the ranch headquarters was a line for him to follow. The line was dotted with a Jeep off to the side, a ranch car in the middle, a Sheriff's department car under a cedar tree, and a truck he recognized as Billy's. He had arrived.

Kicking the rudder pedals and turning the wheel, he went into a wide, banking turn. He eyes roamed the countryside below him finding the two men running parallel to the road on the south and two men walking slowly, rifles held across their chests, toward the disabled ranch vehicle on the north. He recognized these men.

He widened his turn.

#

"John!" shouted the heavier of the two hired hands.

From under the disabled car came the reply. "What? Who is it?"

"Boss man sent us to cover you. You want to get out of there'"

"Throw a few shots across the road and see if you can draw some fire."

Three shots sounded from the posse's position.

No response.

"Now what, John?"

"I'm comin' out. You see anything move over there, you shoot it. That guy can shoot and I really don't aim to be his first human victim."

"Come ahead."

John ran.

#

Juan pushed harder. He had to find the shooter without giving him the advantage. Juan could only assume that the shooter knew the country better than he did, because Juan knew that if he were the one with the 7mm he'd have checked out the entire area well, extremely well, before laying an ambush on probably armed targets that were mad and willing to shoot back. He reached the top of another rise.

There below him was the disabled car. John was running like a crazy man for the bush on the far side of the road. A bee buzzed by Juan's ear and dirt kicked up at his feet. He hit the dirt as the sound of two shots came to him.

#

John dove over a clump of sage and did a neat tuck-and-roll with a half twist coming to rest belly down. .357 pointed in the direction he had just come from.

"Where is he?"

"Atop that rise on the far side of the road," was the response from the two man posse, both of which were digging themselves into the sand like a pair of frantic stink beetles.

#

Lary and Chet heard the two shots and changed their direction of travel.

#

Juan looked around through the scope of his rifle, wondering how the shooter had made it across the road unseen. Then the thought hit him. "Those shots had been too close together to have come from one gun. They sounded different, too. Not heavy enough for a 7mm. "Crap! There's somebody new in this game, Wetback."

He heard footsteps behind him.

The Deputy spun around.

#

Chet said, "I'm going to split the distance between you and the road. You go ahead on this line. Okay?"

"Sounds good to me, just make sure you've got a good target before you do any shooting. Seems like we got a bunch of folks coming in to one spot from too many directions," Larry yelled back.

"Hopefully we have this jerk surrounded."

#

Billy found himself looking down the barrel of the Deputy's rifle. He was so out of breath he couldn't say a word. All he could do was drop his rifle and raise his hands. The sick grin on his face made Juan chuckle.

"Crap! You trying to get yourself killed, Billy?"

#

Ben Beazley sat in the passenger seat of Bud's LTD cussing and mumbling about how slow Bud was driving. "If you don't get a little heavier on that gas pedal, we ain't never goin' to get there, Bud."

"If a hundred and ten miles an hour isn't fast enough for you, I'll get out and you can go on alone. We only got three or four miles to go, so sit back and enjoy the ride and scenery."

Bud was enjoying the Sheriff's impatience and added, "I haven't totaled a car in over year, so you ain't got a thing to worry over except how many bodies we're goin' to find when we get there."

The look on the Sheriff's face changed from worry to just-plain-mad. "Don't talk about bodies."

Bud knew when to shut up,

He drove, braking and downshifting skillfully to make the turnoff. The back end broke loose in the turn and they did a full circle spin before the front of the car was pointing in the right direction. Bud punched the gas, rear tires squealing in protest during the maneuver. The two men came in sight of the disabled ranch car as the speedometer passed 85.

"What's goin' on?" asked Ben.

"Beats me," Bud replied, slamming on the brakes and throwing the car into a slide.

Chapter 5

The seven hunters gathered slowly in the middle of the road next to the disabled car where it all started. Nobody had anything to say as they listened to the plane circling overhead and scanned the country around them with the furtive eyes of prey rather than the sharp eyes of hunters.

Chet reached inside the Jeep and grabbed the mike for the radio. Depressing the button on the side of the mike he said, “That you up there, Artie?”

The answer was almost immediate. “Yea, boss. It's me. What's goin' on?”

Chet started to answer. A beige LTD with the Sheriff's office emblem on the door came in sight hell bent for leather. It went into what appeared to be an uncontrolled spin. Chet was the last of the group to clear the road. He was also the last one behind a big cedar tree.

“Dammit, Bud, just park this thing. Don't try to get fancy,” the Sheriff's smile was back in place as the LTD spun toward the scrambling men.

Bud brought the car to rest against a barbed wire fence on the opposite side of the road from the tree loving crowd. Ben was out of the car before the tires came to a stop and asking questions at the top of his voice. “Where’s the shooter? Why are you all standing out in the middle of the road like ducks in a shooting gallery? Is the shooter dead?”

He watched the faces as the men came from behind the tree. "Don't tell me he just disappeared, again. Seven of you and an airplane, and the man just walked away." He threw his hat on the ground. "Horsefeathers!"

"Where's Juan?"

"Ain't seen him."

#

Sue Garth sat at her own kitchen table while the older woman fixed the tea.

Carrie Martin was doing her best to brighten up the conversation, but so far had failed. It seemed as if nothing was a safe topic of conversation. They all brought tears.

"Carrie, how can I go on married to a real man like Lew when I can't give him the sons he needs? It just isn't fair to a real man like my husband to be married to a shell of a woman like me."

The look on Carrie's face went from a strained smile to a mask of rage, "How long are you going to go on putting yourself down? I'm your friend. I like you. But, I'm getting just a little sick of listening to your sob stories all the time.

"Would you like to hear mine?

"I'm thirty-seven years old and have nine kids. One more in the oven. Does that make me any more a woman than you or my husband any more a man?

"Bud and I belong to a church which doesn't allow us any choice in the matter of kids. We love all our kids, but don't you think it would be a little nicer if there weren't quite so many and we could take a little more time or spend a little more money on each of them.

"What have you got to cry about? I'm sorry you don't have any, but do you think you'd make much of a mother if this is the way you go to pieces. Don't you think it would be a wiser thing to work solving the problem - see another specialist, maybe even a shrink for the depression - than to sit around moping and crying about what a failure you are?

"Your first job as a wife is to keep your husband happy and, if you're fortunate enough, your second job is to bear him children.

Maybe God is just waiting for you to grow up a little more before He blesses you with the splatter of dirty diapers around the house." Carrie slammed out the back door in tears.

The younger woman just sat there with a look of total shock. A fly buzzed through a hole in the screen door and headed straight for Sue's face. She brushed it away, the motion breaking the spell of the moment. She ran to the back door and shouted at the sobbing back standing not five feet away, "Damned if you haven't just hit the nail on the head," She paused, "I think."

The two women met in sobbing embrace, breaking it only to move back into the house to answer the call of the whistling tea pot.

"I'm sorry."

"Don't be. If my best friend won't tell me, who will?"

#

With a sense of a total loss of freedom, Artie set the Piper down on the graded strip at Stirrup headquarters. His smile disappeared. His shoulders fell.

"Someday, I'll fly forever and be free like an eagle."

He killed the engine.

#

The phone rang.

"Si?"

"Tonight."

"Mucho gusto."

"Okay, listen carefully. You will rebrand the cows in one truck and dump them on Stirrup. One truck is for you. One truck goes to the auction yard after you carefully rebrand them to fit the certificates. Understand?"

"Si."

"Bueno."

#

The sun was an hour short of the horizon when Lary said, "Good night," to Chet Handley and started unloading the pickup at Homestead Well.

Chet's reply was, "Will we see you for dinner? We eat at nine."

"Not tonight, thanks. I will use the guest house, though. Don't wait up."

Chet drove off.

#

"There ain't no way you're goin' to get me to fly another load anywhere near that same state for awhile, let alone into the same county. Forget it."

He hung up.

#

Eleven Deputies stood around the room, smokin' and jokin'. The jokes were strained and the laughs were so false that Ben didn't have to speak up when he said. "Have a seat and we'll get down to business."

Silence fell like a wet blanket on a small fire. The ten men and one woman found chairs and sat.

"As most of you are well aware, we have had a killing, a shooting, rustling, another shooting, and an attempted murder in the past twenty-four hours. The last time Apache County was so unfortunate was during the Pleasant Valley War, before the turn of the century. There was a day in the thirties when two men were killed in this county, but they were both crooks caught in the commission of a crime.

"I have just been informed by the Supervisors that this will not be allowed to continue. Seein's as how they won't allow it to continue, our job is going to be considerably easier. All we have to do is catch the fellers that committed these crimes and not worry about anybody committing any future ones, which means we're all out of business as soon as we solve these."

Stopping to take a drag from his cigar, he looked around the room. He went on, "I'm sorry if that was a lousy joke, but I thought maybe I ought to try to lighten things up a bit so you're all thinkin' with me and not moping about things that have happened.

"We're goin' to go over everything we've got for everybody's benefit, right here, right now, and nobody is goin' nowhere until we've come up with some ideas to put a cork in our little crime wave and put the boys that got Oscar away long enough to receive their free shot in the arm from the State of Arizona.

"Let's get the windows open, nonsmokers upwind, loosen your belts, off with the ties, turn on your brains, and, remember, I want everybody involved. If I had all the answers, I'd be here telling you what to do, not brainstorming with you

#

The 7mm sights centered on the brightly lit window of the Stirrup ranch house. Figures of Chet and John moved around the room, rolling and jumping in and out of view. As the fierce, brutal struggle went on in the house, the finger on the trigger tightened to take up the slack.

Chet spun and lashed out with his leg. His padded foot caught John along the jaw bone.

John crumpled to the mat, hard.

The window shattered.

John's abdomen blossomed in blood from his navel to the hip bone.

Chet pulled John out of the center of the room, slapped off the lights, and was punching the buttons on the phone before the echoing sound of the shot died.

"I'll kill that....."

#

"The fat is in the fire now. I think."

The finger on the 7mm calmly triggered off rounds that poked holes in everything in sight that was Stirrup's.

#

The big eighteen wheeler rolled down the highway, tires singing. The trailer was empty except for two men who sat under a swinging propane lamp playing cards, their motorcycles strapped to the sides near the back doors. Neither of the men was paying much attention to the cards.

The truck slowed and turned onto another paved road. The sign alongside the road read. "US 61".

"Where we goin' tonight?"

"Beats me. They tell me nothing, just as they tell you."

"What you want to do, deal or quit?"

"Quit."

"You want the cards?"

"No. They are not for me. The dealer gave them to me only because I had lost all my money at his table. If I still had money, I would not be here this night."

"Busted is a way of life for me. I like the good stuff."

"Si. The good life is the only way, but one must work to enjoy the wine and the Señoritas. Is it not so?"

The man with the cards tossed them on the floor of the trailer and shrugged, "Maybe we will hit it big one of these days, my friend."

"Nobody has hit it big stealing cows," the eyes took on a dark, hard look, "and I am not your friend. As you Gringos say, I am only your associate."

"We'll share a cell if we get caught, associate," he spit out. Strolling to the front of the trailer, he sat down with his back to the wall. A Bull Durham bag and papers appeared in his hand. The other man watched as he rolled a smoke, lit it and, after drawing deeply, exhaled. The pungent odor of marijuana hit the second man's nose, "It will not be good for you to be high on this one. This will be a big haul and we may have to ride the bikes home. You do not ride well after smoking weed."

"This is some primo stuff, got it from a feller over to Holbrook. Want a drag? One stick is all it takes and you can do no wrong."

"No. You will do plenty wrong if you smoke more."

#

Billy heard the shooting at the ranch house as he drove his truck under the gateway to the headquarters of Stirrup. His first thought was to kill the lights on the truck. With his second, he took the AR-15 from the rack, the magazine was still in place from this morning.

Easing the truck to a stop, he killed the engine and opened the door. The courtesy lights came on, startling him. He dove to the ground, kicking the door shut behind him. Lead slammed into the truck just before the light went out.

Billy cussed and mumbled.

A shot rang out from the direction of the house.

Billy watched the dark countryside for a muzzle flash so he could get his bearings on the shooter.

Another shot rang out from the house. Billy caught the flash out of the corner of his eye, as the 7mm slammed into action from the slope beyond the well house in reply.

Billy started moving.

#

Chet wasn't at all happy. John was wounded. The phone didn't work and nobody answered the radio. "A million dollars' worth of equipment and nothing works when you need it."

He jacked another shell into his father's 30-06.

The 7mm spoke.

Chet saw the flash and fired two rounds at it, knowing he wasn't going to hit anything on purpose, he couldn't see the sights in this light. "Maybe I'll get lucky."

He didn't.

#

Trucks pulled off the pavement of US 61 onto a pair of ruts west through the cedars.

#

Lew left the Sheriff's office in a bad mood; it didn't seem to him like anything had come out of the four hours of jawing and thinking. That was four hours he could have been home with his wife. Right now she needed him more than Ben or the county.

He flooded his truck by pumping the gas trying to start it. The battery was just about dead when Bud came out and asked. "Problems?"

"Damn truck won't start."

"Slow down. Smells like she's flooded. Let it set for a spell while we talk."

"Bud. I've got to get home. She needs me and you know it as well as I."

"Lew, settle down. You ain't no good to anybody when you're all excited like this." He was grinning. He knew the truck wasn't going to start, he had pulled the coil wire.

Lew wondered what was going on and started to interrupt, but Bud stopped him with. "Now, you just shut up and let me have my say. You and me go back a long ways. I consider you the best friend I have. Your wife and mine are good friends. As one friend to another, you are going to worry yourself into an ulcer or a grave if you keep it up. Your mind isn't on the job and if you slip bad enough you know that Ben will have to let you go. So let's just settle down for a few minutes and think this through."

Lew rolled a smoke and offered the makin's to Bud. "Nope, you keep'em. Ben asked me to take you with me on the investigation of Oscar's death. He says you got good instincts. We're in this together. Also," his grin growing, "Carrie called. She said you just might want to pick up some flowers or something special, there just might be a surprise waiting for you at home." He broke out laughing so hard he had trouble getting the words out.

"Where am I going to get anything at this time of night? I think both of you have gone bonkers. What are you talking about anyways?"

"This ain't Phoenix, you know. Let's drive down the street and see if there's a light at the flower shop. If there is, I'm sure we can get them to open up for THE LAW. Millard's live right behind the shop and they don't do enough business to turn down a paying customer, no matter what time of night it is. We'll take my car."

#

Lary Ronson took the last box from the bed of the pickup and carried it inside the lean-to attached to the cabin and walked back to the truck. He sat down on the tailgate and called the dog to him. "Well, Crackers, looks like we can call it a day. You must be worn out from chasing all those rabbits. Someday you're going to catch one, and then what are you going to do with it?"

The dog's tall thumped wearily as he stopped panting long enough to lick the man's arm. The man's hand scratched his ear.

Lary's eyes turned to the sky. "I've never seen so many stars at one time in my whole life, Crackers. It's like a big, black canopy with a light behind it and somebody has spent years poking holes in with an ice pick."

Lary moved to the cab and started the engine. After making sure the dog was in, he put the truck in gear and set out for the guesthouse at Stirrup.

#

The rig pulled up to a loading chute. The back doors came open forming a funnel from the chute to the box. The two men fired up their cycles and roared down the ramp after adjusting their ski masks. They both stopped at the gate of the corral feeding the chute. The driver, also in a mask, opened the gate and waved them toward the cab of the big truck. In the distance the sound of heavy trucks broke through the bikes low rumbles.

The man standing next to the cab drew his finger across his throat and both motorcycles died. "This is a big one, boys. We're gonna fill three trucks from here. I will never be able to thank these ranchers around here for building so many loading chutes in so many remote places. We're gonna get rich just usin' them all."

He pointed off to the north and added, "By my information, there should be about four hundred head of steers just over there not more'n a half mile. Move them in this way. There's a spreader fence along this line here." He waved his hand to the northeast.

"Si. I know this place."

"Me, too."

#

Billy lay in the dirt waiting. He wanted the shooter. But, he wasn't sure he was the one to do it. "If he don't do something soon, I'm guessing I'll just get to lay here all night. Whoopee, a camp out."

He moved to get a rock from under his belly. Billy was getting cold and cramped, fast.

#

Lary guided the truck over the ridge into the depression which surrounded Stirrup headquarters. The lights he should have seen weren't there. He stopped, doused the lights and got out of the truck.

Crackers joined him on the road and began watering the sage.

#

Handley fired two more rounds and screamed at the silence, "What do you want? You stupid idiot, John's bleeding to death and you're playing games. I'll see you hang!"

A 7mm round slammed into the wall not two feet from Chet.

He moved.

#

Lary saw two flashes followed by the sound of shots and yelling. A third flash from the hillside and the sound of a shot set him into motion.

Crackers jumped on Lary's leg.

"Boy, you stay. Stay here. I got to get down there."

The dog eased under a clump of sage and lay down, looking whipped. Lary put the truck in low and headed into trouble.

#

Chet was getting madder and more worried about the man on the floor.

#

Lary wished he had a gun bigger than the .22 pistol in the glove box as he continued toward Stirrup.

The old pickup rolled with only a whisper of sound into the yard next to the house. Lary could see the broken glass in the big window. He called softly, "Anybody around?"

"Who's there?"

"It's me, Lary. You okay in there, Chet?"

"I am, but John caught a round. Anything moving out there?"

For an answer, Lary revved up the engine and let the revs die with a rumble and pop.

Nothing happened.

He turned on the head lights as he ducked out the door on the house side.

Again nothing happened,

"He must be gone again. Chet, is John so bad he can't be moved?"

"It's a gut wound and I haven't had time to check it out any further. Your truck bed empty?"

"Yep."

"Come on in and we'll load him up. If you don't mind, that is."

"No problem."

#

Watching the lights go on at the ranch house and two men loading another in the back of a pickup, Billy waited.

#

The flower shop was closed, but the windows of the Millard home were bright and the sound of a shoot'em-up on TV came to the two Deputies as they got out of Bud's car.

"You sure about this, Bud?"

"Have I ever led you astray, my friend?"

"Do you want me to list the times, or will a simple yes do it?"

"Trust me." Bud laughed. "How much money you got on you?"

The younger man dug out his wallet and checked. "Fourteen bucks and maybe a couple more in change," he answered, digging in a front pocket.

"Ain't enough. Here's twenty more. Pay me back when you can." Bud handed the money over and then added. "Get a big, beautiful bunch of whatevers. This is your night. I guarantee it."

"I just wish I knew what you were talking about and what was going on."

Bud knocked on the door.

#

Shef Petty guided his maroon LTD north out of St. Johns toward his area of coverage around the small reservation border community of Sanders. His mind was on all that had been said during the meeting and the fact that he had done none of the talking. His father told him only last week, "When you're the second newest on the force, you keep your mouth shut and learn."

"Well, I kept my mouth shut tonight not because I was learning, but because I didn't have anything to say. I guess I might be learning something, at that. Who am I to tell those boys how to catch the big crooks, I do all right with drunks and the occasional petty thief, but against these organized lawbreakers, I am a real rookie." he thought.

A flash of light off to the left of the highway caught his attention.

Finding a pull off atop a rise, he stopped the car and got out the binoculars.

As he got out of the car, Champ Padilla's voice came over the radio signing off for the night. Shef reached for the mike and asked Champ to stay handy for ten minutes. Champ only lived about three miles back down the road. If this was something needing a backup, Champ would be right handy.

The light flashed again as he centered the glasses on the spot. From the bouncing and flickering of the light, he said, "Bikers."

He watched for over five minutes as the light became two and then one again. "They're covering a lot of ground," he thought.

Champ's voice came over the radio. "Nine to fifteen. You goin' to let me go to bed or do you want me to stand next to this car all night?"

"Fifteen to nine. I got a couple of bikers out here. Looks to be five miles north and a bit west of your place. Back off the highway about two miles or so. Anything out there I should know about?"

"Hope to shout there's something out there. Z Bar has their prime stock out there and there's a catch pen and loading chute to boot. Don't go away I'll be right there. You better scramble the 'Oh, No Squad', I think you found our rustlers in the act."

"Is that the pen Z Bar calls Zuni Cienaga?"

"You got it."

"I'll call it in."

The dispatcher broke in with, "I have all that information, nine and fifteen. Sheriff has rolled. Eight and four are on the way to block two other access roads to that area. Be advised that there are three access roads to Zuni Cienaga from your side, fifteen. The first road leaves the highway at milepost 327, turn is to the west. Units one, four, eight, nine and fifteen shift to channel two, now."

#

The second rig pulled away from the loading chute full of Z Bar steers. Two men stood next to the corrals, talking.

"We're pushing it a bit by taking so many, aren't we?"

"Nope. We don't have much longer to operate in this area and we're gonna get while the gettin's good. No matter how many we take tonight, you can bet the Sheriff will be catching the heat from the Supervisors, the cattlemen, and the little old ladies sippin' and singin' society to put a stop to all this rustling. I intend to get our money's worth out of this place for the chances we're taking before he gets his dander up."

"Three trucks make a lot of tracks and noise and are going to be a lot harder to ease down this country highway we have to use."

"I know, but we could never hit this place again and there are just too many good steers out there to leave any behind for the next guy."

"I still don't like it, especially when I have to drive the last truck."

"What are you griping about? I have to ride with you. Back it in, let's get loaded and out of here."

#

Billy shifted the rifle to his left hand and felt of the .45 in his belt for reassurance. He was scared like never before. "All these years I successfully missed Viet Nam and all the other shooting scrapes and now this. Aggie, I hope you're praying for me. I need all the help I can get." As if the night heard his plea, a dark specter of a man moved over the crest of the rise in front of him.

"I think I've got the tiger by the tail now," he thought, as quietly as he knew how.

#

Lew got out of Bud's car holding the large bouquet of flowers. There were carnations, roses and a funny looking lily type flower all grouped together with sprigs of fern and other greens, tied together with four different colors of ribbon. It was more than a handful for the man.

"Have a nice evening, Lew."

"Somehow I'm beginning to get the feeling I'm goin' to, whether I want to or not. See ya in the morning?"

"Not too early, around nine should do it.," Bud put the shift lever into 'Drive' and said, "Sleep tight," chuckling as he drove off.

Lew walked up the drive toward the front door, noticing dim lights in the window and hearing soft music coming from the house. Hesitating at the front door, he unconsciously checked his shirt tail and shoe shine. "Damn. I'm acting just like a teenager on his first big date."

The front door opened and he was greeted by the sight of his wife in the sheerest of nighties.

"This just may be the start of something for both of us." The purr in the voice overriding the see through she had on. Or, could you call that on?

She reached for his arm and added. "Come in to my darkroom and we'll see what develops,"

He smiled, "Oh, you're a photographer now."

"No, but I'm sure you'll get the picture."

"Yup. Things are beginning to come in focus."

"Let's see if we can make it even clearer."

She turned out the lights.

Chapter 6

"Unit One to all units. Be advised my ETA milepost 327 is ten minutes.

"Unit four cover middle access mile post 325.4 off US 6l. Unit eight cover the north access mile post 335 off US 61. Block and hold both accesses. Units nine and fifteen move to milepost 327 and wait. Over"

"Unit four to one. Ten-four."

"Unit eight to one. Ten-four."

"Unit nine to one. Ten-four."

"Unit fifteen to one. Ten-four."

"Unit one to all units. We should have these boys trapped. If it is the rustlers, they are going to fight, most likely. Don't take big chances. Don't get excited. Remember your training. Get numbers, descriptions and, if possible, take prisoners. If semi's are involved, think back to the reruns of 'BJ and the Bear'. You can't stop a rig with a cruiser and I can't get replacements for cruisers or Deputies.

"Remember, too, that this may just be some kids out joy riding or rodeoing, so don't start shooting unless shot at and keep it cool. Over."

"Eight to one. I'm in position. No sign of fresh tracks here. Ranch gate is closed and locked, two chains and two padlocks. Over."

"One to eight. Ten-four."

"Fifteen to one. I'm in position. This road is wide open over a cattle guard, but there are no tracks of anything bigger than a pickup and no cycle tracks. I can hear a big engine growling in there and an occasional cycle engine whine and pop. It really looks and sounds like the boys we're after. Over."

"Ten-four, fifteen." The Sheriff's mind was working overtime trying to close all the holes and still play it right from the standpoint of the safety of his men and building a case to convict these suckers. He knew that his men were well trained and as ready for something like this as men can be with or without the actual experience. They'd been in many high speed chases, down all kinds of roads, but only one or two had been required to use a sidearm in the line of duty. most were ex-military, and most of them without combat experience.

"I wish we were like them cops on TV. Every one of them gets shot at once a week at least. These boys of mine might be ready for what could be their big one," he mumbled, watching mile post 321 whiz by.

"Four to one. In position. Tracks all over the place. I ain't too sure, but the newest sets of semi tracks look to be made goin' out. They turn north toward the Interstate. Guessing, I'd say at least two eighteen wheelers have come out of there. There's a chain here, so I've strung it across the cattleguard and set my portable barricade in place. The car is sitting across the outside of the barricade, lights off. I'll turn everything on if I see something comin'. Over."

"Okay, four. Don't use yourself as part of the cork. One, out."

#

"That's the last of them. Truck won't hold another. Close the doors and get ready to roll." Jumping off the loading chute, he told the bikers, "You boys will have to ride home on the bikes. Stash them in the trees just out of town like before. We'll pick them up."

He walked to the cab of the truck, climbed up and yelled, "Roll this rig. Let's get out of here."

#

"Nine to one. With fifteen awaiting your arrival. From the sound of things, they are getting set to roll a semi. Fifteen says he hasn't heard the bikes in three or four minutes." Champ looked across the fence to the tree Shef was in, saw him jump to the ground and start running for the cars. "Sheriff, Shef's running this way like his tail's on fire. Looks like something's poppin'. Hold on."

Shef jumped the cattle guard and shouted, "They're rolllng a big truck to the northeast toward US 61. Bikes seem to be following."

Champ calmly passed the news to the other units, hooking the mike when he finished.

Shef was in his car by the time the transmission was finished and grabbed the ignition key just as the Sheriff came back with. "Eight and four stay put. Nine and Fifteen roll, in that order. I'll follow.

"Break. Dispatch - Get the Highway Patrol and ask for roadblocks at junction 191 and I-40, passing no semi's with cattle until further instructions. Contact the New Mexico State and Zuni Police, and inform them of the situation and ask for a roadblock at the border on 61. Over." he put the mike down in his lap, "We may need all the help we can get." He looked up.

"Four to One. Sounds like they're coming my way."

"Max, don't you take any chances, I ain't about to explain all this to your wife. Over."

"I'd just as soon tell her about this myself, thank you. Over."

"Nine to Fifteen. Double check the corrals after I roll through, Shef, and then come on. Over."

"Ten-four nine."

"Nine to One. Doesn't appear to be anybody left at the corrals. In pursuit. Over."

"Be careful, Champ. Over." The Sheriff's voice was both excited and concerned. "All units be advised One is leaving the pavement and in pursuit with nine and fifteen. Over."

"Fifteen to One. If there's anybody left at the corrals, they're well hid. Joining the pursuit behind nine. One, I have your lights in sight. Over."

"Ten-four fifteen."

Max could hear the rig getting closer. The milder scream of the bikes was beginning to be heard as they too got closer to his position.

Juan saw the lights of the truck and two bikes moving away from him and in the direction of Max. He reached for the mike. "Eight to Four. They are definitely coming your way. I just saw the lights of the rig and two bikes. Good thing the moon has gone down, if it were still up, they wouldn't be using lights and we'd be chasing sound and it sounds to me like a tank column comin'. Over."

#

The two bikes screamed down the pair of ruts which led to the highway. They were side-by-side each using a cut as his personal race track. Rounding a sharp curve wheel-to-wheel, they laid over so far that the shoulder of one touched the leg of the other. Both riders' face wore an expression of determination.

"Awright!" shouted the man in the southern rut.

"Rapido!" came the reply from the other rider as he twisted the throttle.

The rider in the northern rut slowly pulled ahead, first by a wheel, then half a length and finally a full length.

#

"Unit one. Be advised the Highway Patrol will have roadblock at US 191 junction with Interstate in approximately ten minutes. They have no units in position to cover south end of US 61 any sooner than forty-five minutes. County unit ten is rolling to that location. ETA five minutes. Zuni Police are stationed at junction of 61 and border monitoring channel four."

"Unit one. ten-four. Dispatch advise Highway Patrol at least two heavy rigs have left the scene here and are headed north. No time estimate available. They may be past that point. Recommend New Mexico stop all heavies and look for beef wearing Z Bar brand. Call out all reserve units. Over."

"Ten-four. Dispatch out."

"Dispatch from Unit One. Get another operator for channel two. Use the jailer if available. Monitor, both channels utilizing the back-up radio. Over."

"Ten-four. Deac is available and coming up on this channel, Stand-by. Dispatch One over."

"Dispatch Two on the air."

"Gotcha. Deac. One out."

"Dispatch Two standing by."

#

"Another quarter mile and we'll be on the pavement."

"If we don't bog this rig in the sand first."

"If we do, I'm walking."

"Well, I ain't digging it out by myself."

Both men laughed.

#

"Unit One. Be advised Z Bar owner Elliot reports north access road from County 4 is washed out. He says there ain't no way a semi is going that way."

"Ten-four dispatch, One, out."

"One from Four."

"Go ahead, Four."

"Ben, it looks like they're just about here. I can see the loom of their lights just over the first rise. Two bikes just crested the hill. Putting the cork in the bottle now. All lights are on. Spot light picking out two bikers coming to barely controlled stops. Mighty heated discussion out there. Ben.

"The two bikes are separating. One going south and one north, both paralleling US 61 inside the fence.

"The truck is now cresting the rise. Air brakes sounding.

"Oh, hell, he's down shifted and hit the throttle. Ben, he's going to crash through. I'm getting clear. Four out."

"Get out of there, Max. Try to take the front tires on the truck.

"One to all units. If they clear Four's position do not, repeat, do not try to stop them. Keep in contact. Sooner or later we can stop them safely at our leisure.

"Eight. Go after the biker heading north.

"Nine. Take the biker to the south.

"Ten. Stay in position. One out."

#

"What?"

"Cops!"

"Don't stop! Stomp it."

"Right!"

The big diesel roared as the loaded rig gained speed down the side of the rise.

"We'll never make the turn onto the highway after crashing through the cop car. This rig will lay over on her side if I try to make the turn at the speed we'll be doing."

"Don't take the gate. At the last minute cut for the road and take out the fence. Four strands of the best barbed wire in the world isn't going to slow this baby down. Mash it. Grab another gear."

#

Juan left his station at the cattleguard after cutting the chains across the road. He pushed the 4 wheel drive Blazer to its limits, cross-country, through the sand knowing that in a chase between a bike and a Blazer, the biker had all the advantages. Except one. That one chance was to put the Blazer alongside the bike and force him into something and to do that four wheels was better than two.

He ran without lights for a mile and a half on the odometer, stopped and shut off the engine. Getting out of the car he listened.

The sound of a single bike far away from the road came to him. The biker was trying to go around Zuni Cienaga and get out the other side.

Juan knew how to stop that.

#

Champ jumped the LTD off another hillock and dodged another tree, keeping the lights on the fleeing biker as he slalomed through the sage brush and juniper trees.

Moonlight gleamed off the bike rider's face as he turned, knowing the car was behind him.

Champ turned on the spot light. The biker noticeably flinched and hunched down over his bike making every effort to get more speed out of the red Honda. As Champ watched in amazement, the biker hit a hillock of sand, flew into the air and came to rest five feet up in a ten foot Juniper.

#

"Four to One. The truck has turned away from the roadblock and crashed through the fence. He is on the pavement heading north toward the Interstate on 191. Four rounds fired by me at the tires with no apparent effect. No return fire. That baby is flying, Ben."

"Ten-four, four. All units not in pursuit of bikers converge on US 191 and Interstate junction. Dispatch two advise DPS and New Mexico of situation. One out."

Ben put the mike in his lap and concentrated on driving along the dirt road.

Cresting a rise brought the lights of unit 4 into view. He reached for the mike. "One to Four. Is the cattle guard clear?"

"Soon's I move the car. Ben"

"Move it!"

Ben watched as the unit moved out of his way. He made the turn onto the highway without tangling in the wire and dug up sand left by the loaded semi. Once on the highway and feeling solid ground again he turned on all his lights and watched the speedometer climb.

His face wore a grin. "I've got you now, sucker." he shouted at the truck in the distance.

#

"That idiot is heading for the road." thought Billy. "If he's got a car waiting. I'll lose him."

#

Champ grabbed a leg on the semiconscious man in the tree and pulled. Quince hit the ground with the sound of a dropped watermelon.

"Let go of me, you dirty . . ." he started, coming off the ground with the most ungraceful haymaker Champ had ever had thrown at him.

Champ let go of Quince's leg and planted his fist in Quince's belly.

"Whoosh." Quince put his hands up.

"Quince, you old drunk, what the hell you got yourself messed up in here, boy? I don't think you're goin' to be drinkin' much for the next few years. You're goin' to be a guest of the state and they don't serve booze."

"You got nothin' on me. I was just out riding my bike for the exercise.''

Quince started laughing. "Oh! What you got in your pockets, Quince?"

#

The truck's speedometer needle buried, "Good thing this is a fairly straight road, huh?"

"You got that right,"

"They're goin' to have a roadblock up here somewhere."

"Probably just before the Interstate. Just before the crossing there's a tight cut. I'd put it there."

"So?"

"This thing got an auto-pilot?"

"Right. Wasn't even an option."

"I guess we're goln' to have to bail out somewhere's along this road. Got any ideas as to where?"

"Yup. Top of the ridge line about four more miles. Them cows in back won't stand much of a chance."

"How about us?"

"Shoulder's soft just past the top. I found that out the hard way one dark night not too awful long ago. Took me four hours and a wrecker to get out of there."

"Okay, You go out first and I'll hit the other shoulder, otherwise one of us hits the pavement."

"That wouldn't be healthy. Let's do It."

"Goin' to be a long walk to anywhere."

"Just so's I can walk in freedom."

#

"One to all units. I am closing the Interstate at a high rate of speed. The suspect truck is ahead of me about a half a mile. Topping Parker Draw in about two minutes.

"Dispatch. Notify Highway Patrol that ETA Interstate is eight minutes. Call Paul Elliot and ask him to come to the roadblock. Get the livestock inspector out of bed and tell him to get out here. One out."

"ETA eight minutes. Elliot and inspector to roadblock. Dispatch out."

"One to Fifteen. Where are you'?"

"Right behind Four on your tail. Fifteen out."

"One to Four and Fifteen. Just follow my play, if I get put out of action, Four you take charge and Fifteen you try to pick me up. If I'm out of it, follow four. One out."

"Four. Ten-four."

"Fifteen. Ten-four."

#

"Comin' up on the ridge line."

"Right. I'll go first and meet you on your side."

The sound of the truck changed as the pedal was released on the rise to the ridge.

"We'll head for Navajo Springs cross-country."

"Get set." The driver eased the truck to the shoulder.

"I'm ready. Good luck." He opened the door and stepped out into the night.

The driver aimed across the road, opened the door, and went out into the air screaming. "Geronimo."

#

"One to all units, topping Parker Ridge, NOW!"

Ben saw the truck nearing the bottom of the draw on the wrong side of the road. As his mind was working on why the truck was on the wrong side of the road when there wasn't a curve for miles, he saw the truck slowly leave the roadbed and start out across country, through the fence.

"Oh, no! There's a deep gully down there. You fool." he screamed.

The truck found the gully.

Chapter 7

Juan raced the final quarter mile to the gate. His body hurt from the jolts it had taken with the blazer going forty to fifty miles an hour over the rough terrain, but with any luck he would get to the gate before the biker.

He locked the brakes and killed the engine at the same time, sliding to a stop in the gateway. Jumping out of the Blazer, he drew his .41 Magnum and cocked his ear for the sound of the bike. The sound he was listening for came to him not from the open country, but from down the highway. He was too late. He jumped into the Blazer and started the engine. The gear shift lever received all his pent up tension as it was jammed into first. His foot slid off the clutch pedal and the car leaped forward only to die just short of the pavement. He tried to restart the engine, telling himself to calm down. The engine was having none of it.

His eyes roved the gauges and found the gas gauge pointing to empty. “You can't be empty, I just gassed up before leaving town,” he said to the gauge.

He got out and looked behind the vehicle. Where he had stopped in the gateway the dirt was wet. Drawing the flashlight from the door pocket, getting down on hands and knees, he examined the underside of the Blazer. The front of the gas tank was stove in and a wet streak ran back from the bottom of the dent.

“Crap.” He had holed the tank. “Two days, three vehicles. The Sheriff will love it.”

#

"I think maybe I will find another part time job, this one is a little hard on my body." The Honda screamed down the highway, its lights out.

#

The three Sheriff's units, their lights flashing, went roaring by the man lying in the low weeds at the right shoulder of the road. The man got shakily to his feet, brushed himself off and hobbled quickly across the highway. His right leg hurt from the knee to his hip. It felt like a muscle bruise, nothing more serious.

"Where you at?" he whispered.

There was no answer.

"Come on. We got to get out of here before those Deputy Dawgs think to look back up here."

No answer.

He hobbled around looking, his leg feeling better with each step. "Come on. Where are you?"

He glanced at the truck which lay bent and twisted, half in the ravine. The sound of bawling, pain wracked cows reached him, but he felt nothing. Those cows were only dollars lost and nothing more.

As he watched, the man from the lead car ran to the side of the cab, climbed up and looked in.

"They'll be coming back here now. Where are you?" he almost yelled.

"Sorry, but I've got to be going," he said loudly, as he ducked through the right-of-way barbed wire fence and started cross country for Navajo Springs, 20 miles away.

#

Ben dog trotted from the cab toward the other two units. The two Deputies met him next to his vehicle.

"The cab is empty. There is no way the driver could have ridden that out and not be in the cab now. The only place he was out of my sight long enough to get out was right this side of the top of the ridge. Shef, you go up there and look around. Be careful."

"Yes, Sir."

"Max, take a look all around the truck and make sure there are no tracks leaving it made by somebody other than me."

"Okay. Ben."

"I'll see if I can get some folks out here to salvage these cows." He reached for the mike.

#

Lew eased his cramped arm. His wife stirred restlessly, her pillow had been disturbed. She opened an eye and smiled at the man she loved. Lew grinned back, his free hand caressing her. He nuzzled her neck before saying, "I think I'll buy flowers more often."

"Might not be a bad idea, but I think it was the nightie."

"Were you wearing one?"

"I was. It must not have been the thing to wear for a long winter's nap."

"Well, it can't be the night before Christmas, something's stirring."

She bit his ear lobe.

#

As Billy worked himself over the countryside, his mind played terrible tricks on him. It was dark enough that he couldn't see much more than the deepest of shadows and large terrain features within about twenty feet, but every once in a while his mind would pick out a shadow and tell him it was the shooter.

The shooter was out there and Billy knew it. He'd caught sight of him twice. Billy wasn't going to give up until daylight, he'd made up his mind.

The foreman worked hard at walking quietly. For a man in cowboy boots with undershot riding heels, walking in this sandy terrain wasn't easy, let alone walking quietly.

Billy stopped.

From ahead of him came the sound of rolling gravel followed by the rattle of the gravel against a metal object. "A can." Billy thought, "We're almost to the road."

Billy hurried on.

#

Using the searchlight, Shef found the signs at the right side of the road where the first man had jumped from the truck, and hit the soft dirt. Something bright gleamed in the light.

Shef picked up a set of keys with his pen. “These haven't been here long, no rust.” he said aloud. He slipped them in a baggie and tucked them in a cargo pocket.

He continued searching.

#

Champ tucked the handcuffed Quince into the back seat of the LTD. He had read him his rights, searched him carefully, and advised him he was under arrest for suspicion of rustling, which due to the number and value of the critters was going to be a big rap. “Quince, you're going to have a long time to dry out, this time. And, it won't be in the county jail.”

On the front seat lay the results of the body search Champ had done. A pocket knife, three dollars and twenty-seven cents, disposable lighter, papers and a Bull Durham sack containing marijuana made up the total collection. The Deputy had tested the contents of the bag and got the brightest yellow possible on the color chart. It was good stuff. Maybe even the stuff they were looking for in connection with Oscar's killing.

He climbed in behind the wheel, started the engine, slipped the stick into 'Drive,' touched the gas and felt the back end of the LTD bury itself in the sand.

“You might as well relax, Quince, we're going to be here for a long while.”

He reached for the mike.

#

Lary was glad it was a warm night. John and Chet wouldn't be suffering in the back of the truck from the cold. It was bad enough, John hurt and all, but at least the cold wouldn't be a problem. He eased the old truck around a long turn and caught a sign that read, “Holbrook 4 miles”. “I hope Crackers is all right.”

#

The dog was where he had been left, resting comfortably, under a clump of sage with one ear cocked for the sound of his returning master.

#

Ben kicked the spent shells out of his .38 into his pocket and reloaded from the speedloader at his belt. These six rounds were the last he had with him. There were at least four more cows that had to be put down.

"Max. You got any .38 ammo with you?"

"Nope. I use a 9mm. You want me to finish off the rest?"

"You better otherwise I'll be empty."

"You got it."

Ben grabbed the mike which he'd left hanging out of the window and said, "Dispatch - One. Where's all them people I wanted out here?"

"On their way, Ben. It took me some time to find the Stock Inspector, but he's on his way, too."

"Get a hold of every charity organization that feeds folks within a hundred miles and tell them if they want some free, emphasize free, beef to come on out and get it. They'll have to cut it up, but it's prime stuff."

"Will do."

"Also, get in touch with that fella in Springervlle with the locker plant and ask him if he wants to buy some good beef cheap and in a hurry. If he does, have him get out here, pronto. And, tell him to bring his tools."

"How many head you got down, Ben?"

"Too many."

Ben saw lights come over the ridge, slowing as they made their way down the slope. In the lights from Shef"s cruiser, he saw the blue pickup and gooseneck stocktrailer of Paul Elliot's. "Paul's here. One out."

"Dispatch out."

#

"Dispatch. Unit 8."

"Dispatch."

"I am in need of a tow. Gas tank is holed. 10-20 is cattle guard on US 61 at mile post 322.4. I am all finished right where this all started. Over."

"Will roll tow truck as soon as possible. Be advised, Juan, there are no other units available to pick you up. Dispatch out."

"Crap!

#

"Dispatch. Unit 9."

"Dispatch."

"I am in need of a tow. Buried in the sand up to my shiny new undercarriage. LTDs shouldn't be called upon to go where no car has ever gone before. My 20 is US 61 approximately three miles south of the southern access to Zuni Cienaga. I am about a mile from the highway. As far as I know there are no roads, ruts, or otherwise, any nearer than the highway. Will turn lights on for locator when you have a unit in the area.

"Also, be advised. I have a suspect in custody. Suspects name is Quince Carter. Possible charges include possession of marijuana, resisting arrest, rustling, failure to carry motor vehicle driver's license, operating a motor vehicle off the authorized roadway, driving under the influence, and others. I think he's going away for a while. Over."

"We'll get to you as soon as we can. Do you require another unit?"

"No."

"Dispatch. One. See if you can get the chopper from the hospital to pick up Champ and Quince. Over."

"Okay, One. Will do. Dispatch out."

"Nine out."

"Hang tight, Champ."

"Will do, Ben."

#

"One from Fifteen. You better get up here, Ben. I got a body."

"Dispatch. One. Get us an ambulance and the coroner out here."

"Will do, One. Dispatch out."

#

"Look, Chet. I have to go back and get my dog. If you don't think you'll need me, that is."

"The doctor said it was just a surface wound. I can get a ride if need be. We'll be another couple of hours and I can get one of the boys at the ranch or even Artie to pick us up. Go ahead."

"You're sure?"

"Yeah. Thanks. Thanks a lot for being there when you were needed."

"Anytime. Hopefully not soon."

The two men smiled at each other before Lary turned and went out to the truck.

"We might just get along after all," Chet said aloud.

The lady behind him said, "Excuse me?"

"Just talking to myself. ma'am."

#

Billy eased down the cut to the roadbed. He could hear the shuffle of feet in the loose gravel ahead of him and saw the specter of the man he was following. The man shaped darkness broke into a trot moving along the roadbed away from him. "It ain't enough I got to walk in these boots, now that sucker wants to do a marathon. Well, you just do your best sucker, I'm right behind you," Billy whispered to the night.

The man ahead of Billy slowly pulled away from the foreman. Billy moved as fast as he could go quietly, but was unable to make up the lost ground. The gap grew until Billy could only just make out the moving man as he passed light colored patches of background.

Billy estimated the distance he had to make up at better than a hundred yards and he was fizzling fast. "I will give up smoking tomorrow," he vowed.

The specter stopped, silhouetted against an almost white patch of sand.

Billy stopped trotting and, as he kept moving slowly, cautiously forward, tried to regain his lost breath.

The shadow of a man appeared to sink into the dirt. Billy dropped, finally remembering the guns he was carrying. The modern day cowboy brought up the AR-15 and lined up on the last position of the specter.

#

"This walking through the countryside alone at night is for the birds. I wonder where that idiot went?" He started singing cadence just to keep him going.

The terrain was flat, but tufted grass and sage kept him stumbling and cussing, mostly cussing.

"I wonder how they got on to us. Somebody must have talked." he speculated again. "It just doesn't make sense that they would just find us without a tip." He stumbled again. A rattlesnake sounded his statement of desire to be left alone by something so big.

"Oh, hell!" The man ran for ten paces before stepping off the edge of a small wash, landing flat on his face in gravel and sand.

Working the sand out of his eyes and mouth, he said, "I'll bet it was the wetback, he's related to half the county, probably blabbed it all over the country how he was making his money. That fat wife of his didn't get much, that's for sure."

He staggered off again, both eyes full of tears and sand. "Now I really can't see. Doesn't make much difference anyhow it's so dark." Lining his footsteps up on the loom of light he knew to be the small town of Navajo Springs, he started singing,

"Over hill, over dale,

We have hit the dusty trail.

As this rustler goes tripping along."

#

Ben watched the back doors shut on the coroner's wagon.

"Broke his neck in the fall from the truck, Ben. That's my preliminary findings. The question is, was he pushed or did he jump?"

"From the marks on the other shoulder back up the hill away, I'd say he jumped after the other man was already out. No sign of anybody around the truck down there, so that leaves just these two. One dead, one walking."

"We'll run the autopsy anyhow."

"Let me know if anything strange shows up."

"Will do. Take it easy, Ben, and I'll see you around."

"Right. You, too, Doc."

Doctor Peters got in the van and started off. Ben turned to Shef, "You stay right here. Don't let anybody stomp out these tracks until I can get Lew out here. It won't be until first light so settle in for a spell."

"Lew can start tracking now, we've got lights."

Ben put a smile on his face for the first time since he'd seen the truck head for its end. "I happen to know that friend Lew has better things to do this night than track some stupid cow stealing sucker across this county. Besides, I want you to work with him and start learnin' the fine and necessary art of tracking. I'll get some horses out here and you two can chase that sucker to kingdom come and nail him good."

"How we gonna get horses through all these fences?"

"Cut them. I'll get somebody to follow along with a 4 wheel drive to patch them up. Maybe that idiot detective the Stockman's Association hired can handle that job, or maybe I'll give a couple of county roads guys a chance to earn their paycheck for a couple of days."

"Okay. Thanks for setting me up with Lew."

"Don't thank me. I just set you up to be called more often than any other deputy on the force, other than Lew. Get some sleep in your car. Lew and the horses will be out here at first light. Lew don't know it yet, but he's got a long day ahead of him."

Ben looked at the wreck, watching Paul Elliot help about fifteen folks cut up his prime steers. Fourteen non-profit organizations and the packing house had responded, "Kinda gives you an idea of the value of good beef steak, don't it," he said to himself, but out loud.

"What's that, Sheriff?"

"Nothin', Shef. Goodnight."

"Goodnight, Ben."

#

Lary rolled the truck to the spot where he thought he'd left the dog, stopped, opened the door and called.

No response.

He started to get out when he noticed something moving in the road about as far in front of him as the headlights were lighting up.

Ears flapping, tongue lolling, belly to the ground, it was Crackers.

Lary got his face washed.

#

The shooter had been out of sight now for about fifteen minutes and no sound had reached Billy to help him locate the man.

Billy felt a rock digging into his belly, but was afraid to move. "He's out there and I ain't giving him a target," was the thought that ran through his mind.

He set his mind to wait it out, one way or the other.

Billy wiggled slightly to ease the pressure from the stone.

A rock rolled ahead of him. It hit something glass with a 'tink'. Billy snuggled deeper into the dirt.

A grunt.

"What the devil?" Billy said to himself.

The sound of a motor firing shattered the silence of the desert night. A headlight stabbed into the darkness. Two revs and a pop backing off and then up from the ground came a man riding a large motorcycle. The three tail lights rapidly disappeared around a corner in the road.

Bill had forgotten he had a gun. He chuckled to himself as he got to his feet. "That's one problem Marshall Dillon never had in Dodge City."

The pattern of the three tail lights still burned before his eyes, two across, and one higher up the middle. "I'll know it when I see it."

He started trudging back up the road the way he'd come, all at once feeling the tiredness in his bones from the hours of tension and fear.

#

"How many of them are left, Paul?"

"SIX! Fifty-four dead ones cut up and gone."

"Insured?"

"Yeah, but insurance only pays average market value and those steers were Prime. I'll only get about 70% of their value. I just hope the company doesn't balk because we've cut them up and given them away." He turned from the carnage and added. "Do you know that fella from the packing house wouldn't take any until all those organizations had what they could use. He even helped them cut'em up and told them to bring them to his place and he'd help them get the beef ready for the freezer at no charge. Don't that beat most ever'thing?"

"Yup. If you need a statement to verify loss let me know, Paul. I'll be glad to help out. You might just be better off claiming them as contributions to charity on your taxes."

"That's a thought."

Elliot turned toward his pickup and trailer. He stared at the trailer with its six occupants, shook his head and left the scene.

"Goodnight, Paul." Ben said to the retreating taillights. To himself he added. "I quit. It's nighty-night time for this old man."

#

Ben woke up a bit later than normal wondering why he dreaded this day. Then he remembered Oscar Billings' funeral was this day. He was supposed to say all kinds of nice things about Oscar, but, "All I want to do is yell at him for being stupid enough to get himself killed," he said to the figure in the mirror as he shaved.

The service drew folks from all over. A representative from the Governor's office was there, as was the President of the Arizona Law Enforcement Officers' League. His pall bearers were three of his sons and three nephews.

The Downtown Chapel of the Church of Jesus Christ of Latter Day Saints was filled to capacity with folks scrunched in tight in the pews and many standing in the hall way at the back. Some of the non-LDS folks were out on the walkway leading to the main door waiting for the journey up the hill to the City of St. Johns Cemetery, where the Billings family had been buried since the first one, Lamar Billings, died in 1884 after a spill from a very rank horse into a rock the same size as the head that hit it. The rock won.

The family headstone was already close to full with the many names of the Billings family that were interred there. The last one had been fourteen years in the past.

After the service was over and the Bishop had said the closing prayer, the casket was carried to the hearse at the curb on the main drag of town right across the street from the funeral home where his body had been prepared and next door to the High School facility that had just seen its last graduating class. The new facility was waiting for September.

The hearse took the lead of the procession down two blocks, turn right up to 4th North street and turn left. After a short journey up a small hill the procession turned right past the city equipment yard and through the wrought iron arch into the graveyard where a few hundred folks who couldn't get into the service waited.

The service at the graveside was short and sweet. Folks lined up to pay their final condolences to the family until his wife of 24 years could take it no more and asked the rest of the folks to wait and catch her when they saw her. She ended with, "Oscar loved his job, all of you, and the Sheriff's department. He died with his boots on and he'd tell ya, it just doesn't get any better than that. I'm here to tell ya, I'll miss that man until my dying day and then I'll get to see him again."

Ben was the last one at the gravesite. "Oscar, why did you do it? All the dealers in the world aren't worth one of you." He turned and went to the back of the fenced area, got into his car, and drove toward his office.

"Dispatch to one."

"One."

"Springerville hospital has a man that's dying from a belly full of buckshot. Somebody left him in a wheelchair at the front door."

"On my way."

The man was dead when Ben arrived. No identification. Fingerprints were taken to find out who the Hispanic man was.

Ben took the fingerprint card, climbed in his car, reported to dispatch, and drove toward St. Johns.

Halfway there he said, "Well, Oscar, you got one with your one shot. Kick him to hell for me," and laughed.

Chapter 8

"Two days and nothing. No rustlers. No shooter. No nothing. My tracker can't find anymore tracks. The grass we got off Quince matches the airport stash, but nothing else on the streets."

"What about those other trucks you were after?"

"DPS says they never hit the junction at I-40. Your guess is as good as mine."

"They must have turned off. Lots of backroads in that country."

"We looked."

"Nothing?"

"Nothing," Ben watched his beer bubble for a few seconds and then added, "and to top it all off, Billy had the shooter in range and forgot he has a gun."

"Quit picking on Billy. He's too good a man to be horrahed because he didn't kill somebody."

"Gimme another beer, Lenny, and then go tell that to the County Supervisors, like I have to in fifteen minutes. Those three are sitting over there in the Court House trying to come up with a way to get rid of me and still solve all these cases. My force is getting just a little too expensive for them."

"Look, Ben, I pay taxes and I hate to see the County equipment get shot up, beat up, or otherwise scratched, dented, or mutilated, but I really don't think those three across the street are out for your badge. They may want some answers and, maybe to see just a little more action, but not your badge. In all the years you been Sheriff, the only hassle you've had with them is over the extra bucks for the

4 wheelers. They're there to watch out for the dollars, that's what we elect them for. Here's your beer."

"Thanks. You may be right, Lenny, but I'm 55 now. They must want a younger man in this job."

"Have they said that to you, Ben?"

"No. But, if I were in their shoes, I wouldn't want an old man in such a demanding job."

"Fifty-five is not the end of the road. Ben, maybe you ought to go up to the Guidance Clinic and get a professional to help you with this thing you have about your age. I'm 61 and still going strong, but I remember what it was like to turn fift,,,."

"Fifty was easy; it's 55 that's the problem. I feel like an old man."

"If that's the way you feel, maybe you had better give the job to a younger fella. We don't want an old man in the job. Sure am glad I ain't old."

Ben gulped down the beer, put the glass on the bar, took his hat from the buffalo horn and said, "One of these days it'll be you that gets old and I won't have any sympathy for you, either." He grabbed a pack of gum from his pocket.

Smiling, he left for the Court House.

#

"Billy, you've got to just forget the whole thing. You aren't a trained lawman and this isn't a time when every man knows how and is willing to use a gun. We hire our gun-toters now days. It's Ben's job, not yours."

"But, Aggie, I could've put an end to this whole thing with a shot in the right place. A leg or a tire would have done it."

"Yeah, and you just might have missed and got yourself killed. Then where would I be with a wedding coming up, all the stuff ordered, and no groom." Aggle picked up a tape recorder and steno pad before adding, "I have to go play recorder at a Supervisor's meeting.

"They're going to get a status report out of Ben. Should be interesting. Ben's big toe is in the wringer for the first time since he's had the job. I wonder how he'll handle it."

"You can bet, he'll want to look as good as possible, Aggie. Somehow, he's got this opinion that he's getting old and may not be able to handle the job anymore."

Billy pecked Aggie on the cheek, took a quick look around the office, and, seeing nobody looking, patted Aggie's bottom as she walked passed him.

"One of these days, Billy, you're going to do that to the wrong girl and get your head knocked off."

"Not unless you do it. I'm done patting other bottoms, Ma'am."

"You got that right, cowboy."

#

Carrie Martin strolled toward the Post Office dressed in a loose shift looking totally content with herself and the rest of the world. As she passed the Bank, the sight before her stopped her dead in her tracks.

Sue Garth was emerging from the Post Office, a smile on her face from ear to ear. Tasteful makeup colored her face. Her dress was colorful, form fitting, and bounced with the spring in her steps. She was greeting every passerby with a heartfelt, "Hello" or "How are you today?" Sue's hair had just been done, a hint of red tint added to her brown hair. Sparkling blue eyes were complimented by gold tone jewelry set with small blue sapphires.

Sue saw Carrie and ran to her. Open arms wrapped around the older woman, lifting her off the ground and twirling her around. "Thank you so much, Carrie. You did what all those pros I saw couldn't do."

"What was that? Yell at you?"

"No, silly. Make me glad just to be a loved woman and take the rest of life as it's handed me."

"You'll get my bill first of the month. And, if you don't put me down, you may need a chiropractor and I may need the obstetrician."

Sue gently returned the mother-of-nine's feet to the solid sidewalk. "Join me at El Charro for something?"

"Okay. Let me get the mail first. Meet you there."

"Okay."

#

Bud stuck his head in the dispatcher's office and said. "Lane, where's Ben?"

"Supervisor's meeting room about now. Can't reach him on the radio, he just went off the air. Why?"

He grinned and shook a ring of keys in the air. "We may have just had a break. I'll be with Ben."

"Right."

#

"Look, Sheriff, there isn't a soul at this table that doesn't sympathize with your position. Everybody in this county wants things done by you, right now. All we called you here for today is a status report. This is not the inquisition or any other sort of an attempt to embarrass you. Can you understand that? We're on your side, believe it or not."

Ben was on his guard. When Mel Hardesty spoke to you in a nice manner it was time to watch your money, stock, and/or daughters. Hardesty was 62 and had been on the Board of Supervisors for eighteen years, constantly being re-elected because nobody had the guts to run against him unless they were totally radical, and in a super conservative area like Apache County, nobody voted for any kind of a radical. The rednecks of Tennessee were panty waists compared to the good-old-boys of northeastern Arizona.

"Mel," Ben began, "and you other members of the Board, these things are being worked on. We're not making what anybody would call progress, but we are working on it. I could blow smoke in your eyes with a lot of bull . . .

"You try that and I will have your badge, Ben." Eddie Yellowtail, a Navajo, didn't believe in mincing the white man's words. He was willing to wax eloquent in Navajo anytime, but in English, short and sweet was his way.

"That's why I'm not going to try. We have no clues to the rustlers except Quince, so far he won't say a thing. Primarily because he's had a steady case of the DT's since we put him in a cell. The doctor bill for his care is in my stack of bills to be okayed by you."

"Along with three or four new four-wheelers, no doubt."

Ben looked over at the third member of the Board. Willa Yashtee was new to the board this year. Her reputation was one of 'If it ain't spent on the reservations it is not going to be spent.' The only folks in the county that liked her just a little bit were those in her district that benefited from her votes.

The Sheriff knew she wanted him out and a cousin of hers in.

"Lady and gentlemen. I've tried everything I know on the shooting of Oscar Billings. My best men are on the case. The Highway Patrol has joined us and so has the Border Patrol. Federal Narcotics agents are just waiting for proof, no matter how slight, of interstate or international transport before they step in. Once again, the only clue is the stash we took off Quince."

Hardesty broke in with. "What about this mysterious shooter. Is that puffed up Handley whelp working an insurance scam?"

"If he is, he almost got killed in it."

"Don't get smart, Sheriff. Just lay the facts on us and we'll all be happy."

"Where do you go from here with the investigation?" Ms. Yashtee put in.

"Where is there to go? Any move we make is better than sitting around doing nothing and probably in the right direction. We keep on doing what we do best, solving cases."

"You are not solving this one," Yellowtail said in almost a whisper. He added, "Would you like me to ask the Navajo Police to help you?" his face void of expression.

"Now you just wait a minute. My force has the highest arrest rate in the state, over 95%. Our conviction rate is also the tops. Some cases just take longer than others. Usually, the more serious the case, the longer the time it takes to an arrest.

"Would you have us make an arrest before we have a case?"

"Oh, you have suspects?"

"Always."

"Again I ask, do you want help?"

"No!"

"The Navajo Nation is always trying to cooperate with you, but you just say No."

"Your Navajo Nation's idea of cooperation and mine are two different things entirely. My men are not even allowed on the reservation, except on request, while your mighty, uncertified warriors go where they please and do what they please. Again I say, no, thank you."

"They just may want to get involved. All this crime is hazardous to the Navajo People."

"You can tell your uppity bunch of know-nothin's to stay on the reservation and keep their meat hooks out of my, I repeat, MY jurisdiction." Ben's face was red, his eyes spit fire and the venom in his voice brought instant total silence to the Board room.

The reporter at the table before the Board scribbled frantically as Ben continued. "I've tried for twelve years to work some kind of cooperation with your people and all I get is Bronx Cheers from your mighty Navajo Nation Council, someday if you ask me real nice, Mr. Yellowtail, I'll tell you where you can put your Navajo Police and if you say please, I'll add directions for the future location of the entire reservation system in this country." He stopped for breath.

"Now, Ben. I'm sure Eddie was just trying to be helpful," Mel put in. His eyes daring Ben to say another word.

"Mel, how much longer are you going to go on pretending you work with these people? They out vote you two to one and all they want are the tax dollars spent where they aren't raised, on the reservation."

"As long as the Supreme Court says 'One man, one vote' and disregards whether or not he pays taxes, I'll work with these fine people for the betterment of this county."

"You sound like you're running for re-election on the reservation." Ben picked his hat from the table, bumping the reporter's pencil, and then added, "If you have nothing important for me to do. I do!" He put his hat on and started out of the room.

Eddie Yellowtail stood up, pointed a finger at Ben's back and said, "I will have your badge."

Ben spun on his heel, walked to the dias, leaned over so his nose wasn't an inch from the end of the Navajo Supervisor's fingertip and said, "I got elected to my office by all the peoples of this county, not just the Navajo. The only way you'll take this badge is off my dead body, a felony conviction, or by a recall election. I challenge you to try any of these!"

The Sheriff turned and stalked out.

The reporter ran for a phone, his deadline was twenty minutes ago.

#

Billy decided against stopping at Lenny's for a beer this early in the day. He didn't want to run into Ben and catch the hard time he'd been dealing out. Instead, he started up the truck and headed for the ranch.

Passing Carrizo Creek he spotted a motorcycle going the other way. He'd been eyeballing every motorcycle he came across looking for the tail light pattern he'd seen on the road. The bike was a big one, "That sucker sounds right." The rider's face was hidden behind a dark, smoked face visor and his body covered with black leather.

He made a U turn and followed the biker, trying to get a look at the plates and/or the driver. The bike turned at the first right. At a stop sign, he saw that the plate was covered with mud. Taking a closer look, Billy could see the finger marks where somebody had purposely smeared mud on the tag. Excitement was like charged electricity running through him loading him with power. Billy flipped open the glove box and laid the .45 Peacemaker on the seat next to him.

The biker made a right turn.

Billy followed.

The motorcycle lurched ahead.

Billy hit the gas.

The biker hit the brakes and his left turn signal came on.

"The lights! It's the right kinda bike. I've got that sucker this time." He laid the big gun in his lap as he made the turn and accelerated down the dirt road after the bike.

#

Bud Martin met the Sheriff just as he emerged from the Court House with, "Got some good news for you, Ben."

"About time I got some good news. Whatcha got, Bud?"

#

Eddie Yellowtail was the first of the Board to find his voice, "I move we fire that man," he screamed.

"Seconded," came from Willa.

"Right now I'd almost like to go along with you, but what the man said is true, Eddie, and you know it. He has to be recalled, convicted of a felony, proven mentally incompetent, resign or die. I'm not too sure about his mental faculties after that outbreak, but he hasn't done any of the others." Mel Hardesty knew the law and liked to let others know that he knew the law.

"I withdraw the motion, but I'll have his badge."

#

The biker knew Billy was after him. He'd heard the hard time the Sheriff was passing around about Billy and knew how close he'd been to discovery on that last night raid. Billy wasn't about to shoot him, but once the foreman knew who he was, it was all over. "I will not go to jail. Stirrup must pay." He twisted the throttle to the stop.

#

Tonio shook out a loop, twirled the rope over his head once and laid the noose down over the steer's horns. Taking three dallies around the saddle horn, he signaled the horse to back. The rope came tight. Still the horse was told to back. Slowly, ever so slowly, the big steer was pulled loose from the mud bog.

The big critter had been lucky. This was the first day Tonio had been carrying a rope. He also carried a Stirrup branding iron. For the first time since he'd been working for the ranch, he was expected to work as a cowboy along with riding fence and providing security.

The steer was pulled onto dry land before Tonio stopped the horse and then moved him up to slack the rope, giving the rope a deft flip he loosened the loop over the horns. The second flip freed the steer.

Watching the steer, Tonio coiled his rope.

No cowboy worth his pay would take his eye off a critter that had just been released from a rope. Critters had a nasty habit of taking out all their frustrations on the first thing they saw move. Mr. Chet's father had been killed when he got off a horse, removed the rope, and turned his back on the cow to walk away. The cow had stomped the man into a bloody mud hole before Chet shot the enraged half-ton of beef.

The steer lay on the ground gasping for air. Tonio flipped the knotted end of the rope across the steer's flanks. The exhausted animal made no effort to get up. Tonio rode the horse away about fifty feet, dismounted looping the reins around the horn. That way if the steer wanted to get feisty, the horse would be able to move, and if Tonio hit the horse's back in a hurry they could both move out of there, fast.

The hand walked cautiously to the steer. He prodded gently with the pointed toe of his boot into the spine of the steer. The steer swung his head, rolled the whites of his eyes and bellowed.

"I must get you on your brisket, Señor Vaca or I think you will lay here and die."

Ever more carefully, Tonio worked the steer onto his brisket, legs folded back naturally, the way a cow likes to rest. Tonio surveyed his work noticing here was a problem with the brand. It didn't look right. He knelt and scraped the mud away with his hand.

"What is this?"

Pulling a knife from the sheath at his belt, he shaved the branded area. The Stirrup brand stood out clear; unfortunately, it was superimposed on another brand. Tonio traced the two brands with his fingers until he could tell which lines were for which brand. The brand on the bottom was an L/. "Why would the Señor put his brand over the top of the L slash? This is not legal."

Then he noticed that the top brand was not done with a stamp iron, but had the lines of a running iron. "Who do I tell of this?" he asked the steer.

#

Lary parked the truck in front of the house.

Chet Handley met him before he got to the door, "I just dropped by to see how John's doin'."

"Doin' as well as can be expected after you've had your abdomen laid open with a 7mm round. He should be coming home in a day or so."

"Good. How are you doin' without your bodyguard?"

Chet reached behind him and came out with a Browning Automatic. "I got my bodyguard." He chuckled as he put the gun away and added, "Besides, there are two men sitting on the hill tops watching every approach to this place. Haven't had an incident since John was shot. I think the shooter got scared. He almost killed somebody. An inch deeper and John would have bled to death before we could have done a thing for him."

"New tracks on the road beyond my place. You know, where the gate used to be."

"Sheriff's boys?"

"Could be. Didn't see them, just heard them. Yesterday afternoon. Three or so."

"Want to stay for lunch? Got some fresh trout in."

"Talked me into it. Never could pass up trout."

#

"I move we file a formal complaint against the Sheriff. One copy in his county record and another copy for the Governor." Eddie Yellowtail wasn't giving up.

"Seconded." Willa Yashtee was for anything against a white man.

"I vote no and I want that to be stated in the letter and the public record. Do you have that in the minutes, Miss Albright?"

"Yes it is, sir."

"The vote is two to one in favor, Mr. Hardesty." Eddie was pushing. "Will you not join us?"

"No, Mr. Yellowtail, I will not."

Willa asked, "And why not, Mr. Hardesty?"

"Because there is a lot of truth in what the man said." He waited for that to sink in and then added, "I do not agree with his timing, method or style, but I do see a lot of truth in his words."

"Mr. Hardesty, you may have just ended our working relationship."

"Mr. Yellowtail, I intend to file suit to stop any county monies being spent on the Federal Navajo Reservation. You and your people are always milking the cow, but you feed her mighty danged little. I'm done babysitting you and your people."

Willa found her voice, "The day you file that suit, you will find it difficult to fund anything in this county. We are in a position to control every vote. That will not work in your favor."

"Ma'am, war is hell. Where will you be when the land owners of this county start paying their taxes into an escrow account under protest and I get an injunction against all spending on the Navajo Reservation pending the outcome of the suit?"

He left the room without adjourning the meeting.

#

Bud waved the keys in Ben's face and said, "Lookie what I got. Yeah, the keys from the jump site. Do they tell you anything?"

"Yeah. Jingle, jangle, jingle. Look, Bud, I'm not in the mood for games. Tell it to me straight and let me go kick my backside around the block."

Bud fumbled through the ring of keys, held one up and said, "This key is an illegal duplicate of a Post Office box key."

"Find the box!"

"Find the box?" Bud replied weakly.

"Get Juan to find the box!"

"Yes. Sir." Bud turned and walked off.

"Thank you, Bud. Hang in there," he tried to sound cheerful.

Bud turned, the smile back on his face. "Right."

#

"Look, there is no reason to keep looking around for any more tracks. There aren't going to be any with this wind. Let's go home."

"Ben isn't going to like this, Lew."

"Shef, Ben understands that tracks are not permanent. We haven't had a solid, positive track in a day, and we are just wasting time standing out here holding onto our hats with our eyes on the blowing sand."

"What's next, Lew?"

"A good night's sleep after all the reports are filled out." Lew's face stretched into a smile. He added. "You get to do your share of them."

"Me, a novice tracker, I wouldn't know where to start."

"I'll let you do them all as part of your training."

"I pass. My share is enough."

The two men walked to a pair of grazing horses, removed the hobbles from their front legs, and mounted.

Playing out a game they had begun during the searching, Shef said, "Let's went, Cisco."

"Vamanos, Pancho!"

They were three miles from Navajo Springs.

#

Sue was sipping her coffee and Carrie was checking through the pile of mail she had retrieved from the box when Aggie walked through the front door of the café.

"Aggie, over here. Lots of room for one more," Sue said, waving her hand.

Aggie approached the booth, smiling, "Pretty soon I'll be an old married gal like you two. Guess I'll have to get used to the kitchen table conferences."

She sat down and then added, "What brings you two out of the kitchen?"

Carrie replied, "If I don't get out now and then, I go bonkers. I still got seven kids at home six of them never shut up and the other one always needs changing or feeding."

"Who's watching the team?" Sue asked.

"Grandma Martin. One of the benefits of having the in-laws living next door."

Aggie's face took on a serious look which the other two women noticed. She caught herself, tried to cover up with, "Any secrets I ought to know about a Honeymoon?"

"Just do what comes naturally. You'll do all right."

"Yeah, you love him and he loves you. That's all that matters on the Honeymoon. All the rest will work itself out. Not to worry."

"I'm not really worried. I've waited a lot of years for Billy to get the bugs out of his britches so he would be ready to settle down. I just wish this shooter thing wasn't in the middle of our lives."

"Billy shouldn't be worrying about the shooter. That's a job for our husbands, not Billy."

"Tell him that."

"Think he would listen?"

Maria came to the table and got in the middle of things with, "This a private meeting, or can any woman get in?"

"Sit," chorused three voices.

As Maria slid into the booth, the smile on Aggie's face slipped again.

Maria asked, "What's the matter, Aggie? You should be the happiest one at this table. If I could find a husband, I would be jumping for joy in the streets, specially, if I was loved as you are loved."

"It's just this shooter thing. It bothers Billy so much, and ..." her voice faded.

"What is it?" Sue asked, the compassion in her voice louder than the words.

"You're amongst friends, Aggie. We can't help if we don't know what the problem is," Carrie added with a voice full of concern.

Aggie's eyes got watery and her voice was just barely controlled as she responded, "I just wish my folks were here to see this day. My father said Billy and I would marry someday. Mom agreed with him. That was so many years ago, they said we would be happy. The last words my mother said to me were, 'You keep Billy at arm's length until he's ready to settle down, ya hear'. That was just as they drove off for the weekend they never came home from."

Four pairs of eyes shed tears as they hugged each other.

#

As Billy passed the dump cutoff in pursuit of the bike, he wondered how long the chase was going to last. He took his tally book from a breast pocket of his jacket and opened it on the seat next to him. With a pen from the same pocket he started writing notes as he fought the truck through a wide S turn.

Sparks flew from the bike as the rider laid the bike into a right turn. A furtive glance over his shoulder confirmed the presence of the truck still on his trail.

"The man will be like glue. I think."

"Come on, you sucker. Let me get close enough to blow your tires off. You ain't getting away from me now," Billy screamed out the open window of the truck.

He watched the biker make another right turn at a stop sign he didn't stop for. "He's headed back to town." Billy grabbed the CB mike.

The biker gained ground on the open paved road they were now on and Billy wasn't getting any answer on the radio. A mile short of town the bike turned into the road to the cemetery. Billy followed, almost losing the truck as the back end broke loose in the gravel.

"Dead end road, sucker!" Billy checked the position of the 45, shifting it slightly.

The biker slewed the bike around the first grave markers and picked up the perimeter road, kicking dirt and gravel into the air. After traveling around the cemetery to the back side, he ducked the bike behind the maintenance building and killed the engine on the big bike. He listened for the truck.

Billy fought the wheel through the turns, barely controlling the truck, so busy watching where he was going that he lost sight of the bike. In front of the only building around, he stopped and shut off the truck. He listened for the bike.

Getting out of the truck, Billy grabbed the gun. Seeing fresh tracks of a motorcycle going behind the block building, he brought the pistol up and followed.

Billy rounded the back corner only to be confronted by a man standing next to the motorcycle. The man was apparently unarmed and shaking his head with a look of extreme sadness on his face,

Billy's gun hand slowly drooped as he stared at the rider of the bike.

"You? Why?"

"He is my father, but only uses my mother, and he will not know me. I am sick of being the bastard child. He must suffer as my mother has suffered, as I have suffered."

"Who?"

"The man you work for, Billy. The raper of the county. He would have the biggest ranch, the biggest herd, but not a Mexican woman for a wife and a mestizo for a son."

"You? Chet's son?"

"They have kept it the big secret for all these years. He promises to marry her when the ranch is built. He makes no promises to me. He does not even acknowledge me on the street or at the house. I am as dirt to him."

"Is it right to give hate in return for this? Is it right to take revenge on cows for what a man has done"

"Who speaks of hate? I speak of getting what is my right, a father. If not a father, then whatever I can for my Mother."

"Try the courts, but this is wrong. The way you're going won't gain you a thing, except jail."

"The courts will just say my mother was another wetback working her way to the top in this Anglo world on her back. Remember, Billy, the courts are controlled by Anglo men who also like the hot blooded women from south of the border."

"I could help you. It's not too late. Nobody has been killed and I'm sure Chet will drop all charges when he finds out how you feel." Billy had forgotten the gun in his hand.

"I am sorry it is you, Billy. I like you."

As shock registered on Billy's face, Miquel's hand came up filled with a small derringer. Billy stared at the two little holes the end of it as they spit flame. A tearing flame tore at his chest and abdomen. His eyes lost focus. Billy Cranston fell into the dirt.

Miquel reloaded the Hi-Standard 22 Magnum, put the fired cases in his pocket, and returned the gun to his hip pocket before dropping to one knee before the body of his victim. "I did like you, Billy. You were one who did not look down on me. You even gave me work."

He collected himself, closed Billy's eyes, crossed himself again and returned to the bike.

He started the bike, moved it onto the gravel, and returned to the scene and, grabbing a push broom from the building, swept out all the tracks except Billy's. This took him more time than he wanted to spend, but he went over the area twice to make sure. Miquel again crossed himself as he said a final farewell to Billy settling into the seat of the bike.

Careful on the throttle, Miquel eased the big bike along the gravel road to the pavement, praying the whole time that no one would see him leaving the cemetery.

On the pavement he sobbed, "Adios, Billy," as he twisted the throttle wide open.

Chapter 9

"County Sheriff's Office. May I help you?" Lane said, putting her coffee cup down and grabbing a pencil. Without thinking she also glanced at the tape recorder to make sure the call was being recorded.

"He is dead," came the frantic, barely understandable words over the phone.

"Who is dead? Please calm down and just tell me the whole thing as clear as possible." She cut in the speakers in the Sheriff's office and the squad room.

"The Señor is dead."

"Okay. You just answer my questions. Where are you?" Lane hit the switch calling out the EMTs and Ambulance.

"'He is at the cemetery."

"Which cemetery?"

"The Holy ground of San Juan."

"Who is this speaking?"

"Teresa Salazar. I am scared. I have never found a man dead before."

"Do you know who the man is, Teresa?"

"Si."

"Who is it, Teresa?"

"Señor Billy."

"Billy Cranston?"

"Si," she sobbed into the phone.

"Where is he in the cemetery?"

"Behind the only building, next to the plot of the Mendoza Family.

"Hang in there, Teresa. I have the ambulance and a Deputy on the way. Did you touched Billy or anything around him?"

"No. There is blood everywhere and I could not see him breathe. I have prayed over him. The Priest should be there for the Señor."

"I'Il call him."

Lane reached for the mike, "Billy Cranston down at the Catholic Cemetery," and saw through the window three cars roll out of the parking lot. She returned to her caller. "Where are you?"

"At the Church."

"The Catholic Church?"

"Si."

"Please wait there for the Deputies, Teresa. They will want to talk to you."

"I will wait."

"Do you want me to keep talking to you, Teresa? Or, can I hang up now?"

"You are busy. You hang up. I will wait and pray for his soul. He was a good man."

"Adios, Teresa."

"Con Dios."

The phone went dead in Lane's hand.

She grabbed the mike and called, "Who's rolling to the cemetery?"

"Unit one to the cemetery, Dispatch." The tears in the Sheriff's voice told of the long friendship with the victim.

"Unit thirteen following the Sheriff, Lane,'' Ben would want Bud Martin on this one.

There was no third call-in. Lane called out. "Who's in the third car?"

A moment of silence, Ben broke in with, "Who is that?"

Another bit of silence and then. "Ain't nobody here but us chickens, Sheriff. You will need a chicken to direct traffic or something, won't you?"

"Deac, of all the dumb ... On second thought, you might as well come along and direct traffic. I can always use another deputy."

"I'm your man, boss. Ain't nobody in that jail for me to watch, anyhow, except Quince, and he don't count for nothin'."

"Just don't tell anybody and don't expect to get paid for stealing a department vehicle." Ben paused and then added, "Leastwise, that's what you'll be charged with if you dent that car."

"Okay, Sheriff."

"Ambulance just left the garage, Sheriff," Lane broke in.

"Ten-four."

#

"Well, girls, I hate to break this up, but I'm working and if I don't get back I won't have a job much longer."

"When you and Billy tie the knot, are you going to quit?"

"Haven't really decided. I wouldn't know what to do just sitting at home, never learned to like the game shows and soaps."

"You get used to them."

"Yeah, they kind of grow on you."

"So does mold."

"Wish I could get to watch a few, but this joint ties me down a bit. Worse than a batch of kids."

Aggie laughed as she left the café.

#

Three bottles of Scotch a year wasn't a bad price to pay for the use of a County phone whenever it was needed. It wasn't too often that it was needed. But this one time made it all worthwhile. Roy Carson had been a reporter with the St. Johns Herald for six years and this was the first time he had been in a position to argue his Editor out of a deadline. He didn't have to argue very hard once he'd outlined the story to him. He and the Editor would share the byline because the Editor said there wasn't time for Roy to come in and write the story. Roy figured there was a good chance for this one to be picked up by the wire services, at least within the state. This whole reservation thing was going to come to a head one of these days.

The last thing Roy's boss had said was, "Go get some follow-up. Interview the people. We've got at least three issues of headlines here, don't blow it."

Roy sat the phone in the cradle, looked up and saw Supervisor Yashtee coming from the meeting room. He thought to himself. "As angry as she always is you'd think she was there when Kit Carson rode into Canyon de Chelly and the Navajos were moved to Bosque Redondo. She'll make more headlines with that mouth of hers."

He went after her.

#

Tonio talked to the horse for three hours before he decided he would tell only Cousin Juan of the double brand.

"He will know the way of this, caballo. Madre Dios, I hope he will know."

#

The phone rang three times.

"No! I told them no."

Thirty seconds later it rang again.

"No! I told you before. I will not fly for you again."

"Would you like to die?" The voice was familiar and calm.

"No."

"Tomorrow night at seven. Big Valley strip."

The phone buzzed in the pilot's ear.

#

"Deac, block off the access road. No one in or out except the ambulance. Any questions, call me."

"Ten-four, Sheriff."

Ben's car rolled down the graveled road. For the first time in his career as a law enforcement officer he really didn't want to arrive on the scene of a crime. There had been times when he hadn't looked forward to it and times when he'd have preferred a sharp stick in the eye, but never a time when the dread of what he was about to see was so overpowering. His mind raced through the good and bad times he and Billy had shared.

Ben rounded the last turn before the maintenance building. He eased the Ford to a stop fifty feet away from the block building.

As he stepped reluctantly from the car, the sound of the county's four wheel drive ambulance came to him. He looked over his shoulder and saw the red and white vehicle turn off the highway. Reaching inside, he pulled the mike to his lips.

"Dispatch, the ambulance is here. Deac, nobody else gets in here. Bud, get your camera goin'. Over."

Bud's car pulled gently alongside with Bud brandishing a camera through the window and nodding his head.

Ben let Bud take the lead with the camera clicking in his hands as they approached the body on the ground. Ben rounded the corner. The body of his friend came into view. He lost all control and rushed to the crumpled form.

"Deac, whichever deputy comes next, send them to the Catholic Church to pick up Mrs. Salazar.

#

"Stick it in. Try to turn. Pull it out. Crap! This life as a Deputy sure is exciting. Yes, Sir, Deputy Vasquez, you just go stick this key in all the Post Office boxes within one-hundred miles. I ain't asking you to do this to punish you. Somebody has to do it. Crap! And, of course, you can't put another car in the shop from the inside of a Post Office. Stick it in. Try to turn. Pull it out. Crap! Four thousand, three hundred and seventeen tries in four P.O.s."

Juan wasn't altogether happy with this assignment, but he kept the clerks smiling with his, "Stick It In. Try to turn. Pull it out," and various other comments.

"And only 23 more P.O.'s to go."

He moved over a step and. "Stick it in. Try to turn. Pull it out. Crap!"

#

"How do you feel about the Sheriff, other than what happened today, Ms. Yashtee?"

"Why the peoples of this county elected that bigoted, incompetent rowdy is beyond me."

“Yes?” the reporter said aloud. He thought. “Most things are way beyond you.”

“Do you remember the shooting incident at the Pine Flat Trading Post last year,” she continued.

“Yes, ma’am, I do. Why?”

“Well, that sorry excuse for a law officer never did anything about it.”

Roy thought, “Of course, it was on the Rez and out of his jurisdiction and the Navajo Police won’t let him on the Rez even for a fishing trip.”

#

The ambulance slid to a stop. The attendants set to work. The first jumped out of the side door, a stethoscope and small satchel in hand, running to Billy’s side. The second came out the back door rolling the stretcher. On the stretcher were a blanket and a big fishing tackle box. The driver ran around to help with the stretcher.

Chuck Bradley plugged the stethoscope in his ears and put the other end to Billy’s chest. At the same time, the fingers of his other hand went to the victim’s neck. A look of complete concentration settled on Chuck’s face. The look changed to surprise and quickly to concern. “Get Doc on the horn, Jimbo, this man is still alive.”

The driver jumped back in the vehicle.

#

The phone rang, once, twice, a third time.

“I’m coming. I’m coming.”

She ran into her office, grabbed the phone and said. “County Recorder’s Office, Aggie.” Her face got white. Her knees buckled. She fell into the chair. The phone hit the floor.

After a few moments, the phone in the next office rang.

Chapter 10

"Stick it in. Try to turn. Pull it out. Crap! I can't take this for another day, my wrist is killin' me. Crap!"

#

"I don't know what to do. I've got my six senior deputies working on heavy cases, two shootings, a dope drop, and a shooter of cows. The six remaining deputies are trying to hold down the normal caseload which is too much for thirteen. There are private citizens watching the landing strips and flat spots in this county. Umpteen zillion citizens call hourly asking how long this blood bath will continue, and all I can say is, 'we're working on it.' I don't like the position."

"Well, Sheriff. If you can't stand the heat, get out of the kitchen."

"Go to Hell." Ben stated flatly, to the Navajo Supervisor.

"Again, I offer the help of the Navajo Tribal Police."

"Again, I politely say no thank you."

"It's your neck."

"It's been stretched before."

"Enough, Ben, how is our friend, Billy?"

"He lives. The doctors say that living through this first 24 hours is a good sign. They have him stabilized. Tomorrow or the day after they will operate to put the rest of his gut back in place and catch anything they missed last night. He'll make it. He's too tough to die. And, thanks for asking."

“I guess we are both humans just trying to do the job the way we see is best. Have a good one, Sheriff.”

“Goodbye.”

#

“What, do I do now? Billy not dead and them looking for me?” The motorcycle fired up and roared down the highway. “I will do something they will remember for a long time.”

#

“Look, we have a pickup to make at Big Valley airstrip tonight. What’s the bitchin’ all about?”

“Where’s the boss?”

“Beats me, He hasn’t called or anything in the past three days, but this one is all set up and we don’t need him.”

“Still, I don’t like it. He should be here.”

“Let’s do it right. Then, when he gets in touch, we can show him how well we did it and hit him up for a bigger piece of the action.”

“Let’s get that damned pilot on the phone and make sure he’s scared enough to show, I don’t want to transport that stuff on the ground.”

“Right!”

#

John wasn’t walking too well. He looked more like a meditating monk than a bodyguard as he left the hospital. His hands were crossed over his stomach and he was hunched over as if in deep thought. He must have been an old monk his steps were short and shuffling.

The days in the hospital hadn’t been kind to him. He appeared flabby and extremely pale. He felt flabby. He felt weak as a kitten. John didn’t like either one of those feelings. He had never experienced either feeling before in his adult life. He silently vowed he would never feel those feelings again.

“It is going to be different, me guarding you and getting you into shape, John.”

“You don’t have to do that, Boss. I could always go to my sister’s place in Phoenix and then I won’t be a bother to you.”

"No bother," Chet rubbed his chin and looked over at John. "I didn't know you had a sister in Phoenix. I thought your sister was in Denver."

John stopped walking and looked up, "She was, but she moved."

"Oh, that explains it. My memory hasn't been the best lately anyhow."

"How's the hunt for Billy's shooter going?"

"Nothing new. Ben and the boys are bustin' their buns on this case but getting nowhere."

"I had expected something by now."

"Ben did too."

"How about the rustlers?"

"Nothin' there either."

"Must be tough on Ben."

"It is, but he'll get over it."

#

Aggie Albright sat on the chair in the sterile room looking at her man. His breathing was rough and filled with catches. His color was a ghostly pale green like he had been whipped by a mob or some such group, with dark bags under his eyes. Every once in a while his eyelids would flutter slightly, but no other movement. He just lay there. He was still alive and for that Aggie was overjoyed.

"Billy, you just get yourself well. We got us a wedding to do. I have postponed it until you're ready, but it is still on. You can't get rid of me now."

#

Tonio enjoys Coke. He enjoys Coke like a lot of people enjoy chocolate. Some days he just couldn't get enough Coke.

"Juan will be here soon, I think," he said to himself as he pulled another red can from the cooler on the seat beside him and popped the top. "And then I will tell him of the brands."

#

"Look, I've told you before I will not fly for you again."

"I take it you are ready to die."

"How you goin' to kill me when you can't find me? And, if I see one of your ugly mugs, I go to the Attorney General."

The phone buzzed in the caller's ear.

"Looks like we transport on the ground."

"He picked a fine time to get a load of guts."

"Yeah."

#

"I quit for today. One more key hole will drive me crazy. I ain't far from there now."

Juan put the key on his ring and hooked the bundle on his belt loop. Climbing into the oldest car the department had, he started the long journey home for his meeting with Tonio.

He was already late.

His radio stuttered loudly with his call sign. "So much for Tonio today."

#

"Lane, get the coroner on the horn. I need to know what's going on with that body we found. Nobody sits around this long without identification in this day and age. That cowboy probably has a rap sheet a mile long.

"Also, find out where Juan is and why he hasn't found that PO box yet. Tell him he ain't on vacation and if he cares a fat rat's patootie about his job, he'll get busy.

"Remind Juan not to so much as scratch that old clunker I gave him."

"Okay, Sheriff. Juan's on his way home from Pinetop, the coroner is still out of town, but Bud is looking into the dead man, and four hundred scratches on that old piece of junk you gave Juan wouldn't show and you know it."

"Yes, ma'am, I just needed to do something. I'm so sick of nothing breaking for us I could spit fire."

"I've noticed and so has everyone else. Go have a beer and calm down. Everybody's working."

"Yes, ma'am!"

#

"Look, Roy, I can't print this trash Yashtee gave you. There is nothing to what she says."

"Boss, it's not what she says, but who's saying it. I have it all on tape so she cannot deny a single word. Print it! She is a County Supervisor, and what she says will go a long way toward everybody getting the idea she's all so much baloney."

"No way! Ben has been a friend of mine for quite a while and I don't want to see him slammed around like this. Roy, she may be in a position of power, but that gives her no right to say anything she wishes. Just because she says it doesn't make it true."

"Wait a minute, Boss. This feud between the two Navajo Supervisors and the Sheriff, with the one Anglo Supervisor solidly in the middle may just bring this one-man-one-vote decision of the Supreme Court to a head. As long as the folks on the reservation pay no taxes, but vote to decide where the money gets spent we're looking at the reverse of the situation in 1776. Somehow it needs to get settled before another revolution gets started, and I know a few folks ready to start the shooting if they get taxed anymore to support our red brothers up north."

"How is crucifying Ben with this woman's angry words going to do all that?"

"Folks just may realize how much power those two Native American supervisors have and how hard a time Mel Hardesty has trying to keep the peace and get anything for the non-reservation part of this county."

"I'll run it," the editor said, "but only after I warn Ben, and after he and I discuss the reasons for running it."

"Fair enough. You're the boss."

#

Miguel took a look at the turn off. Not much there but scrub sage and juniper. The sage was thick in this area and he knew how easy it was to hide in the four to five feet high plants when they were packed this close together.

A shadow flickered over him as he leaned against the cycle. Looking up he saw a golden eagle soaring a few hundred feet up. He stood still, watching, hoping the eagle would not suddenly take off.

The large predator was lovely to watch in its freedom as it gently, effortlessly hitchhiked on the afternoon currents of heated air rising from the desert floor. The bronze feathers appeared translucent in the late afternoon sun and outlined the bird in a brassy glow.

"Free from worries and a halo, too," thought the fugitive. "I will never have a halo, but I wish more so that I was free from the cares of this earth as this eagle is. He must only worry about the next meal, while I now must worry about all my foes."

The eagle continued to circle the area looking for that next meal, or maybe just enjoying the free ride furnished by the thermals as Miguel continued to mope. The cars wooshing by on the highway did nothing to break his train of thought. The broiling afternoon sun made no inroads in his mind. Again and again the flicker of the shadow passed over him, reminding him of the freedom he would never have.

He thought of how it had all started, getting even with the father who refused to acknowledge him. Making this man hurt the way he had hurt time and time again. Making this gringo hurt the way he had hurt his mother over and over again. Making the suffering even on all sides after all these years he had suffered.

He had taken the job offered through Billy only to learn how to hurt the father the most. It was easy to find out that the only thing the father cared about was money and that stinking collection of cows and windmills he called a ranch.

How could he love a ranch so much? Did a ranch love back? Could it keep you warm on a cool fall evening? Would a ranch comfort you in your time of sorrow? How in the name of all that was Holy could a man love a ranch so much that he neglected the woman he professed to love and the son of that love? How?

To Miguel it made no sense. That his blood should come from the blood of this man was a further mystery to Miguel. He could not understand how he could love people so completely and things so little when this source of his blood and genes loved things so completely and people so little.

Again the shadow flicked past. Again Miguel thought of the freedom expressed in the eagle. Again, the desire to be free like the eagle ran through Miguel's mind. How could he be free? "If Billy dies, I will never be free," he cried out loud.

"My friend, is there some way to be as you are? Free," he shouted. "I would have your spirit and live forever on the winds of this desert."'

"If Billy lives I will also be in jail for a long, long time. The gringos will have no mercy on one who has shot up one of the rich ones, one of the powerful ones.

"That will not happen."

The seed of an idea had come into Miguel's mind. A seed watered by the years of intense hate and fertilized by the fervent quest for vengeance.

The eagle tucked in his wings and dove.

#

"Lenny, what do ya hear?"

"Nothing but orders for beer, Sheriff."

"I sure do wish something would break pretty soon."

"Not in here. Replacing broken stuff eats up the profits fast."

The phone rang and Lenny walked the length of the bar to answer it. "It's for you, Ben."

"Thanks."

Chapter 11

"Yeah, this is the Sheriff."

"This is Show Low hospital, your gal in dispatch gave me this number, would you please get a hold of Bud Martin for us and inform him that his wife, Carrie, is in the ER here having a miscarriage. She is also hemorrhaging to the extent that we have begun a transfusion. If at all possible we need him here NOW."

"I'll get right on it. Is this life threatening?" Lenny's ears perked up at the seriousness of Ben's tone.

"Yes."

"I'm on it."

Ben ran to his car grabbed the mike, "Unit 13, Sherriff."

"13."

"Where are you, Bud?"

"61 just past Concho headed for the Y."

"Keep on going to Show Low hospital, lights and siren. Carrie's there and it's serious. Hate to tell you this on the radio, but she's having a miscarriage and is bleeding. They have a transfusion running. Work through dispatch and connect with the ER. I'll be right behind you twenty minutes or so."

Ben could hear the siren going when, "Rolling," came over the speaker. The next thing he heard was, "Dispatch, 13, patch me through to Show Low ER on channel three."

"Dispatch to channel 3. Patching."

"Dispatch, One, show 13 and One 10-7. I'm on my way to Show Low. Contact Lew and let him know I am out of touch and he is in charge pending my contact."

"Dispatch, 10-4."

Ben hung up his mike, looked carefully around, and pulled into the right lane, hitting the gas, chirping the tires as he reached for the lights switch.

#

"Hey man, you got something I could take for these shakes. I need a hit, man. You can't leave me here in this cell to die like this." Quince looked like he felt.

"Look, Quince, you been declared detoxed and safe. So just shut up and leave me alone." Deac was never a man with a lot of sympathy for his inmates.

"Deac, I need some stuff man. I'm jonesing like crazy. I can't take it."

Deac looked around and checked the sweating, shaking Quince through the bars. His face was flushed and his pupils were big. "Well, Quince, I could talk to the Sheriff. If you would tell me your sources and who the other rider was he just might be willing to negotiate with you on the matter of your drug needs. Then again, he might say, 'no.' Never can tell."

"What do you wanna know?"

"Who was the other rider?"

"He'll kill me."

"You just told me you were dying without the drugs. Looks like both ways you die."

"Not if I get the drugs."

"No name, no negotiation with the Sheriff. I guess you gonna die, Quince. Sorry about that. I'll try to say some nice things about you at your funeral, might have to lie a bit though."

"You won't tell anybody I told, will ya?"

"Not me, I will just tell the Sheriff."

"Mariano Alverez. Couldn't ride a dirt bike worth beans. Always thought he was better than me, just because he didn't use on the job."

"You sure it was Mariano?"

"Yeah. He was always spouting off about the dope was gonna kill me if I didn't kill myself driving stoned first. Where you think he's gettin' all the money he's been spending."

"I'll let the Sheriff know this and we'll see what he does. Now, who's your source for the dope? Don't lie to me. We will check it out before anything comes your way."

Quince looked around, "Can anybody else hear us?"

"Nobody here but you and me, Quince."

"Man named Ross. I meet him at the Concho Bar on a Thursday evening if I need him. He moves around to different places on a schedule so's he can meet all his customers. Pretty nice guy, don't sell to kids or stuff like that. Gave me credit one time because I needed a hit and was broke."

"You know who he gets the stuff from?

"No. Ain't nobody tells you where they get it. I told you what you wanted, now get me some stuff."

"Got to check with the Sheriff before I can do that. I told you that. Want some coffee to tide you over?"

"Not really, but it'll help 'til you can talk to the man."

Deac went for the coffee with a large smile on his face. "Sheriff, I have some news for you," he said to the empty hallway.

#

Miguel looked down on the ranch headquarters from the highest spot around. Checking to insure that no sun would reflect off his binoculars first, he started scanning the grounds carefully with the glasses. If he could find just the right spot, he could put a real hurting on the ranch and the man who was his father in a biological sense only.

"I am tired of pussy footin' around. Time to get real serious. It don't make no difference what I do, Señor Billy dies and so do I."

#

Sue fell into the chair of her living room just as the scanner picked up the call to Bud. "Not Carrie! No! How can her loving God do this to her?"

She jumped up and grabbed her purse. Thirty seven seconds later she, too, was speeding down the highway toward Show Low.

Inside the house her phone began to ring.

#

The two men climbed into the cab of an old truck. The sides of the truck were a very faded U-Haul orange or whatever color you call their paint scheme, the tires were questionable as far a tread went, and the trail of smoke could be seen if you looked.

"What airstrip they coming in on tonight?"

"Awe, that one down by the lake. You know over the hill to the west and just out of sight from the highway."

"Yeah. I never did like using that one. Only one way in and one way out, unless you have a plane. Who's the pilot?"

"Some rooky clown I never heard of. I'm not fond of new faces around here right now."

"I got my .45."

"We don't need another killing. We'll get the needle cocktail if they catch us for the last one. Killing a cop just doesn't get good advertising with the folks. Even the users are leery of buying after a cop killing."

"But, they still buy. They need, so they buy. That need is what keeps us in business."

"Amen, brother, amen."

The driver made the right turn off 61. "A couple of miles to go now."

"Where we hauling the stuff?"

"Flagstaff."

"We're not traveling on the interstate, are we?"

"Nope. We'll take the ranch roads to the highway just south of Winslow, turn left and then up through Happy Jack on Lake Mary Road into Flag."

"Good."

"We finish this haul and get our pay check, I'm outta here for a place I know in Montana. Wanna come along?"

"Sounds good to me. I got nothin' here to keep me here. I was looking for a job when I found this one."

#

"She doesn't answer, Lew."

"She probably heard on the scanner and is rolling. Thanks for the try."

#

Police officers running through the ER are not a strange sight, but when it is an Apache County Deputy people take notice. Stopping at the desk, Bud asks, "My wife? Carrie? Carrie Martin?"

"She is in the isolation room, room 3. But you can't go in there."

"I'd like to see you try and stop me."

The nurse behind the counter regrouped, "Let me put it this way. If you want your wife to live you will wait for the doctor that I will get right now."

"Oh. Thank you, nurse."

"I'll be right back, and you're welcome."

Bud stood at the counter fidgeting and looking around. He had been in this room many times, a few of those times with his own kids. A broken arm here, a sprained wrist there, but never when it was a matter of life and death within his own family. In one quick moment all his movement stopped. His head dropped. "Father, don't let this woman die, I love her. Please?" he whispered.

A calm settled over him. He knew she would live. How he knew he did not know, but he knew.

A graying man in a white lab coat came out of a door not too far away and moved in his direction. Sticking his hand out, he said, "My name is Dr. Hodges. I am your wife's attending physician. Let's go have a chat for a moment or two."

"She'll be okay, Doctor. I know it."

"She will be fine physically, but I worry about her mental state right now. She is hysterical. Can you tell me why?"

"Other than the loss of the baby, there is our religion. We believe that our children are given by God and the more you have the more you are blessed." His voice was calm and solid like he was on the witness stand.

"Okay. How do we tell her this child was malformed and would not have survived?"

"Just as you put it to me, tell her straight out. She's a cop's wife. She wouldn't want you to beat around the bush."

"How do I tell her she must have an emergency hysterectomy due to the hemorrhaging and she will never have any more babies? That's another question and the most serious one."

"Same way. Doctor, we have nine kids at home already. This one was a real surprise." Tears formed in Bud's eyes. "We both wanted him. But more, I really don't want any more. The blessings sometimes are more than we want."

"Let's go talk to your wife. You will need to tell her that."

#

"You see the plane?"

He looked around the sky again. "Nope. Don't hear one either."

#

To himself the shooter said, "I wonder what they keep in that metal building. There are lots of tracks to it, but it is set well back from the rest. It would not be explosives or anything flammable. The flammable stuff is in the old tool room near the barn. I ought to know, I used enough of that paint when I was a worker on my father's ranch, thanks to Billy. And, I returned that favor by shooting him."

He moved around the back of the hill to get in a position to check out that metal building without being seen by the lookouts he had spotted.

#

"Carrie, I love you. We can weather this just as we have been able to all the problems we have run into."

"But, they want to cut the woman out of me. No more kids."

"Is that a bad thing?"

She looked at him like he was her worst nightmare. She began to speak and stopped.

"We have nine, honey. How much more can we be blessed?"

"We have been blessed haven't we, Bud, nine of the greatest kids in the world. But, we lost this one."

He continued looking into her eyes as he added, "Now it's time to take care of you so you will be around to bounce all the grandbabies on your checkered apron."

"Yeah, I guess you're right. But, my baby. . ."

"The doctor tells me he wouldn't have lived. We'll see him again."

"Yeah, Bud, we will."

"Besides all that, the surgery just takes the factory and leaves the playground in, or so I've heard." He smiled and squeezed her hand.

"You would think of it that way wouldn't you?" Her smile grew.

#

"I hear a plane." He pointed to the south.

"Hit the headlights and light up this field." Both men ran down the length of the field setting cheap battery lights at 100' intervals along both edges of the field. They didn't make it half way when the plane rolled to a stop next to them.

"Special delivery," came the shout from the cockpit.

One man ran for the truck while the other reached for the door on the aircraft as it began to open. When the door hit the dirt the man looked up into a twelve gauge pump shotgun being wielded by a dark man in camo coveralls who said, "Good evening."

"Who are you?"

"No, the question is who are you?"

"Trinity."

"Upwind."

"Okay, start unloading." Bales began rolling out before the voice died out.

#

"Ben, thanks for coming." Bud's hand was stretched out.

"My condolences at your loss. Where's Carrie?"

"In surgery. They just rolled her in."

The two men sat and stared at each other.

#

Aggie sat in the recliner next to Billy's bed. Nothing was changing. The same numbers showed up on the monitor now that had been there three hours ago, and three hours before that, and three hours before that. She was bored, worried, tired, stretched thin, and just plain lost and alone.

#

A shadow of a figure carrying a large rifle slid along the side of the building heading for the small door.

"What is this? Nothing on this ranch gets a padlock. Why here?" The building was only twelve by twenty. The tin sides were not stout enough to slow anyone down for long if they wanted in. But, it would make lots of noise if a person tried to break in.

Miguel moved to the back of the building. Noticing the screw heads were on his side of the wall and remembering his multi-tool was part screwdriver, he proceeded to take the wall apart, one screw at a time until he had a big enough access to get an arm in the building.

"Smells funny in here, like marijuana, and I wonder what else?" Hands trembling, he pulled the covering off of a corner of the nearest bale. He grabbed a pinch of what felt like weeds and sniffed it. Marijuana! A tyvec bag was also in his reach, so he borrowed a bit of something from the bag. Crystal!

"Daddy dearest, I have found your secrets. This will bring you down like nothing else I could ever do."

Carefully, Miguel replaced what he had removed, weed, baggy and screws. And then he ran, ran like he had never run before.

#

They watched the plane leave in their rearview mirrors as they rolled down the dirt road to highway 61.

Chapter 12

"Bud, did you ever wonder what happened to the rest of the trucks on that big rustler job. One crashed at Parker Draw, but where did the other – at least two – trucks go?"

Bud thought for a while gazing around the sterile, palest green waiting room and responded, "No. I really haven't. I've been working on the two shootings, in particular, Oscar's. Just haven't given much thought to trucks. Guess maybe I should have from some respects. Why do you ask?"

"Oh, come on, Bud, four big crimes going on and a man of your abilities having not thought of any of them except the shootings." Ben held up a cigar and pointed outside.

"Naw. No cigars for me, you know that."

Ben pocketed the cigar and sat back down on a brown imitation leather chair.

"But, I have thought about all these problems together. I don't think we have more than two problems going on here. The shooter of Billy and Stirrup ranch are one and the same. Just before I headed over here I got a call from Phoenix telling me that the tire and shoe prints are a match, which is what I thought. That's one.

"Oscar and the drugs are obviously tied together by the drugs. Find the drugs and we have the killers, all four, by the casings we found. Or maybe just two, each with a rifle and a pistol. I really think four. If it were only two they would have had to shoot with both hands at the same time to splatter Oscar the way they did. Four panicked shooters would do just what we saw."

He looked at Ben with a twisted grin before adding, "So, the question is what do each of these problems have in common? The first is Stirrup Ranch. Second one is the drugs. My feeble mind says that the drugs are somehow connected to Stirrup Ranch, either by location or by personnel. Is the shooter trying to keep people away from places on the ranch? Doesn't appear to be. Just about every spot possible has been shot up.

"Maybe, Stirrup Ranch is the drug headquarters. I find that hard to believe, having known what a health freak Chet is and John stays by his side all the time. One of the hands? I don't know."

"That leaves just the rustling as a standalone, or is it?" Ben grabbed a cigar and went outside with a very strange look on his face and walked with determined purpose. He had perfected that walk as a Sergeant in the Corps.

Bud stood and said, "Maybe I will join you. Outside, that is."

#

The sunset was beautiful as Lary and Crackers walked carefully through the sage and cedars away from their cabin at Homestead Well. The dog kicked up his heels to let Lary know he was enjoying himself. Lary reached down and put another collar on Crackers.

Crackers got real serious, real fast.

#

Aggie looked out the window of the hospital room in time to see Ben and Bud enter the smoker's courtyard.

She ran outside.

"What are you two doing here?" No one answered.

"Come on, give. What's up? Somebody die or something?"

By the time Ben finished telling her, Aggie was hugging a tearful Bud and crying down his shirt front.

"Just what we all need, your loss piled on top of everything else. I ain't sure this town will take much more of a beating like this."

"How's Billy, Aggie?"

"Doin' well, the Doctor says. That one slug is very close to his heart, but the doc says the x-rays still show a fair sized gap there. We'll know more tomorrow when they take it out, if he is strong enough then. He lost a lot of blood and they been filling him up. He has a hard blood type to find. Last pint came from Los Angeles, along with two more."

"That's all good news. When he comes around we will need to talk to him. You can tell him when the wedding is before we do that. That ought to perk him up."

Aggie got a bit weepy eyed and reached in her purse for a tissue. She did a bit of tidying up and gave Ben a feeble smile. "I hope so, Ben."

She turned to Bud, "When will your wife be out of surgery?"

"It could be anytime now. They said they would page me if I was not in the waiting room or out here."

"Well, folks, the county awaits its senior law enforcement officer, namely me. So, I will be heading home to subdue the forces of evil. While I am at it I will be thinking of the two of you and the struggles you're going through.

"Aggie, your boss says you have lots of leave time coming so just stay here with your man.

"Bud, I don't care how much time you have coming, so you be with your wife and the both of you get well."

"Okay, Ben. Thanks. Boss, I'll keep you posted. And, thanks. Thanks a lot. Let me know if anything breaks."

#

"Boss, how about we help Ben out now that the news is in print about his terrible job rating with the Board of Supervisors. Let me go undercover for the paper to expose the drug trafficking in this county.

"I'll go out and buy drugs. We'll document all the buys and turn all the drugs over to Ben along with the info on the buys. If I can find just a few pushers and distributors in this county we could put a real crimp in their business.

"What do you think?"

The editor looked Roy right in the eye before he spoke, "Are you stupid, or just have a death wish. You got any history of drugs?"

"No."

"Why would you be buying now? That's the thought that will go through the mind of every druggie in the county if you start asking questions."

"I have two good friends who are users and make no mystery of it. I could ask them to introduce me to their contacts and teach me how. They're gullible enough to believe I would want to use just like they do."

"Are you gonna use?"

"Only if I really have to for a cover. I don't want to."

"Okay, one buy and then we discuss this operation again. I don't want you dead."

"Great. We agree on that, I don't want me dead either."

#

Ben arrived at his lonely apartment shortly after midnight. He had stopped at the courthouse to say howdy to dispatch, check the arrest list, check the jail, and then moved on to Lenny's for a nightcap just in time for last call.

"Good night world, do not disturb me until seven, preferably PM.

#

"What do you mean it's not running right?"

"Just listen for a moment."

The sound of a slap, skip, and putt was faint but it was there. The driver stepped down on the gas and the knock could be heard even more. "We got a lot of hills to climb before we get to Flag and this old buggy just might not make it."

"Let's get as close as we can and then stash the truck in the woods. I have a buddy in Flag with a truck we can hire to move this crap the rest of the way."

The truck coughed and sputtered.

"Sounds like a plan."

#

Reaching down to remove the collar, Lary scratched the dog with his other hand. After chomping down a treat, the dog started romping like a puppy again.

"Well, Crackers, doesn't look like our neighbors are squeaky clean, but we can't prove it yet. Got to find the stash if we are gonna burn'em."

The two of them headed for the cabin and a bit of sleep before another day began for them around 10 AM.

#

Two elk ran across the road, illuminated by the head lights, as the old U-haul truck lumbered north on Lake Mary Road south of Mormon Lake, the only natural lake in Arizona. "Watch out," the passenger cried.

"Tell the elk that." The driver took his foot off the brake and stepped on the gas. No response. The old truck would maintain, but not accelerate. He backed off and slowly added pressure on the pedal. The response was slight, only a mile or two an hour.

The driver started looking for a pull off. "Don't look like we're gonna make it in this rig. Help me find a spot to hide this sucker."

"Oh, great. Just what I always wanted to do, hitchhike into Flagstaff after stashing a load of weed and speed. Maybe if we pour some of that meth in the tank it will take off."

"Ha, ha. Very funny. That's our bonus for this run. Speed freaks don't care where it comes from, they just want it. Now."

"Over there," the passenger shouted. "You're gonna have to back up. You missed it."

The truck crept back at a mile or so an hour until they found the pull off. It was even slower going in the two ruts between the trees until they heard a car go by, but could not see it. "Far enough." The driver jumped out after killing the lights. The engine died as he hit the ground.

The passenger reached over and tried to restart. It was not interested in starting. This was all they were going to get out of this machine.

They locked it up, walked to the highway, hung a handkerchief on a limb to mark the spot, and started walking. The first sign they saw said 'Flagstaff – 30 miles.' "Sure hope we get a ride."

#

A car rolled up the road toward Flagstaff not ten minutes after the men had abandoned the truck. Seeing the hitchhikers, the driver stopped and offered a ride, if needed. Needless to say, the two of them took him up on his offer.

#

The green forest service truck rolled north on Lake Mary Road toward Flagstaff and home. It had been a long night. Some nut at Blue Ridge Campground tried to burn the woods up. Trey was the first one on the scene and had the fire 80% whupped when the first pumper truck showed up an hour later and took care of the rest. He had been asked to stay and make sure there were no flare ups. The license number of the trailer leaving the campground just as he arrived had been given to the Deputy Sheriff and, from the tone of the radio, the owner of the trailer was not a happy camper. A Deputy had caught him just short of Strawberry on his way back to his Phoenix home.

The man tried to deny ever camping in that campground, but his wife said, "Fess up, dear. You blew it," and that was the end of that.

Trey was soot from head to foot. The elk were bad along this stretch of road and the puny lights on his old truck did not give him much warning. Three more jumped out, causing him to swerve to miss them. His headlights reflected off of something ahead in the woods. After stopping and backing up, he found the truck, a truck that smelled of the stuff he had smoked a few times as a teen. "Dang, dang, dang." He knew he was in for an even longer night.

#

Just as the two men were getting out of their free ride to town, three law enforcement vehicles went ripping around the corner through the red light of the signal on the corner with lights and sirens flashing and screaming. The two men decided they were leaving the state without going back.

#

Ben awoke to the ringing of his phone.

"Yeah, this is Ben."

"Sheriff, this is Will, we found one of the cattle trucks at the auction lot in Holbrook. Checking it out now."

"How'd you do that? That's out of our jurisdiction."

"Navajo County Sheriff's office called in the tip."

"So, what do we know about the truck?"

"It's empty. Treads on the tires appear to match the ones we have from the corrals and road. Looking for the driver as we speak. Manager at the lot just came in and said the driver was at one of the motels in Holbrook. One of his hands gave the driver a lift last night and the manager is now trying to contact the cowkicker and find out which motel. Then we will move in with Navajo County boys."

"Okay, Will, keep me posted. I'll get a shower and be at the office."

"Roger that, Boss. Catch ya later."

The Sheriff sat the phone in its cradle. "All right, we may be getting somewhere now."

Chapter 13

One Apache County Sheriff's car and one Holbrook Police vehicle pulled quietly into the Teepee Motel parking lot while a Navajo County Sheriff's cruiser moved down a side road to the rear of the motel grounds. The Holbrook Police Officer entered the office and rang the bell.

A yawning attendant stuck his head out the door to the rear of the office, "Yeah, I'll be with you in a minute." Seeing the officer standing there, he added, "Whatcha need, Tommy?"

"You got a truck driver here, delivered to you by the sales yard around eight last night. Ring any bells?"

"Yeah, he's in Teepee 6. Said he wanted the quietest room in the place. Told him we didn't have rooms, we had Teepees. He took Teepee 6. Didn't have much of a sense of humor."

"Is he alone?"

"Far's I know."

"May I have a key, we need to talk with this gent, Al?"

"Not without a warrant, but let me get dressed and I will escort you with a master key in hand. How's that?"

"Works for me if you want to get in the middle of a gun fight."

"Been shot and shot at before. Viet Nam." The attendant turned, "Let me get my shoes on."

The officer looked out the window at the motel, once again dazzled by the idea of having a motel made up of phony looking teepees each painted like some drunk brave had been given three different colors of paint and told to have at it. Each Teepee had an antique car sitting in front of it. The cars were all 1940 thru 1960 models. A few of them worth a lot of money, like the '56 Corvette he had been coveting for the past three years, but Al wasn't parting with it for any price. Not that he could afford, anyhow. He had been raised in Holbrook and this place had been here as long as he could remember.

Al returned jingling some keys, "Let's go. What did this guy do to attract so much attention, Tommy?"

"Looking for some trucks involved in rustling and someone thinks this guy might know something. That's all."

"Yeah, tell me another one. Three cars for an I-just-wanna-talk-to-you meeting in a motel parking lot. Sure."

The two men stepped into the parking lot, the two deputies exited their cars, the police officer held up one full hand of fingers and a single finger on the other hand side by side, and they moved toward Teepee 6. Behind the back line of Teepees the third deputy moved to cover the rear. He noticed that the window on the back of the Teepee was very small and appeared to be painted shut.

The attendant knocked on the door when the police officer gave him the nod.

From inside came, "Leave me the hell alone. I need some sleep."

"Need to talk with you, Mr. Owens. The sale barn just called and needs some info on your load."

Tommy gave Al a thumbs up.

"What? I don't have a load until tomorrow."

"They are on the phone in my office."

"Transfer it here."

"Can't do it, the control box is out. I have the hand held here and it appears to be working. Just open the door and I'll hand it to you."

The sound of locks being turned was followed by the door opening, revealing a man in his skivvies, put everyone in motion. Al jumped to the side away from Tommy. The Police Officer grabbed the man's wrist, jerking him out, spinning him to face the wall of the Teepee. "Hands against the wall, feet back, and spread them."

The driver complied like he had done this all his life.

"Wha?"

One of the deputies ducked into the Teepee.

"We just want to talk with you, Mr. Owens." The officer reached around and checked the waist band on Owens' skivvies, stepped back and added, "Let's go inside and chat, shall we?"

Owens, one police officer, two deputies and the attendant entered the Teepee. Owens got the only chair after he pulled on the pants handed to him by a deputy after they were checked. Apache County Deputy Will Connor began the questions.

#

Around 8 AM Billy stumbled in his breathing, the monitor went off, and two nurses hit the room running.

Aggie came awake with a start, "What's going on?"

"You need to leave the room now, ma'am. We'll let you know when we determine the problem and the doctor has been in."

Another alarm sounded as Aggie moved toward the waiting room. "I wish my mama was here to hold me."

#

Miguel reached Sanders just as the sun made its presence known over the ridgeline at Houck. Having stashed the rifle in the sage brush a mile or so out, he didn't look any different that all the other darker skinned folks wandering around the little crossroads village.

He knocked on a door.

"Si?"

"It's me, Barto, let me it. I need a place to sleep for the day."

The door swung open revealing a very large Navajo gent in shorts and wife beater under shirt. "You can have the couch until I get back from Gallup around noon. Then I got business here and you will not be welcome."

Miguel went right to the couch and crashed. By the time Barto had the door shut he was out.

"Good night, my friend."

#

The livestock inspector finished his tour of the stock sales corrals. The cowboy with him looked at him like he was crazy.

"Why are you looking for stolen cattle here? You know we check every brand against the certs you guys issue before we allow them to be placed in a pen. This don't make no sense."

"Yeah, I know all about your procedures," McGee looked around some more trying to see any critters that looked the quality of the ones that had been stolen. "I have to admit only once have I found a questionable cow in this place. But, it turned out the iron had slipped in the branding and the brand was splotched all over the shoulder of the poor critter. Let's check that large pen over there with the fifty or so head in it. They're angus and that's what we're looking for, about fifty plus head of real good angus."

"You're going to be disappointed. That might be 57 head of angus, but they ain't real good stock. Just burned out old cows that'll probably end up at one of the burger chains."

"We'll look anyhow."

"I get paid by the hour. Let's go."

#

Maria hung the clean, ironed shirts in her son's closet and something on the shelf caught her eye. Reaching up, she took down the strange shaped carton and read the words, "Large caliber rifle powder."

She reached up and took down a small green plastic box which also had a label, "7 MM Magnum reloading dies, carbon steel." Her mind ran rampant with ideas about the so called 'Shooter' out a Stirrup Ranch. She remembered hearing that this shooter was wearing 9 ½ size shoes. Reaching down she picked up a boot from the floor of the closet, 9 ½.

"Not you, Miguel. Not you. Why would you do this thing to Stirrup?

"We will talk of this when you get home, my son."

#

Bud looked at his sleeping wife, his tears slipping down his unshaven cheeks, and again thought of how fortunate he had been to land a beauty like her. Her looks had little to do with her beauty, it was very much everything about her that made up her beauty, from her physical looks to her heart of love all the way to the day to day strength she had to keep up with a cop for a husband and 7 kids still in the home, or as his mother had put it, "10 kids, but one is a bit older than the rest with more expensive toys." She never complained. She never cried unless one of the kids was really hurt. She lived what she believed, and he needed all those things to keep him stable and focused.

"Lord, bring my wife comfort and peace in all of this. Thank you." He prayed again.

#

"Okay Sheriff, we know nothing new. This driver only started driving that rig day before yesterday. Told me the boss told him that if he left a truck and walked away from it like the last driver, he would put a contract out on him. Not to kill him, but to chain him inside a cattle truck for about a week.

"I got a call into the trucking company to give me a call A S A P so's I can get whatever info on the previous driver they might have. I have a feeling it isn't going to be much and what there is of it will be phony."

"Alright, Will. Get the particulars from the driver and then head on home. You done good."

"Thanks Sheriff."

'Wow! Kudos like that don't roll off Ben's tongue easily. That was almost as good as a pay raise to Will. That ought to even up for the screw up on the two drunks he mishandled last month,' he thought.

#

The two nurses worked over Billy as the alarm kept up its angry cry next to the bed. One of the nurses reached for the panic button just as Billy's heart quit trying. The alarm went into a high, obnoxious mode designed to wake the dead.

Twenty minutes went by with two doctors joining the effort, until, slowly, with reverence, one of the nurses covered Billy with the sheet as the others silently, with heads hanging in failure even though they had done everything humanly possible, left the room and scattered to tend to their living patients.

#

Carrie sobbed in her sleep.

#

John worked out with Chet. Chet pulled the punches and kicks due to John's recent injuries, but John worked Chet over until Chet said, "Enough. You're leaking."

John looked down at his belly, "Guess I am. Didn't even feel the pull." He probed the long stitched wound, "Only one stitch pulled a bit. Nothing serious. I ain't about to baby myself, it just ain't me."

"Good. Still enough. I have work to do. You get rest and get well."

"Sure, Chet. Whose gonna load the truck?"

"I guess that would be me."

#

Maria waited for her son who was sound asleep far away. Tears ran down her face as she thought of the son trying to ruin the father. She cried out to her God and made promises again. She had never kept them in the past. Something whispered in her ear telling her that Chet was using her and had for over twenty years. He had even required that she repay the loan that started the café.

She tried to call Chet.

No answer.

She thought of the café being closed. Folks would think she was sick. They would come over to the house and find her a mess. Starting for the shower, she fell apart and fell on the bed, sobbing.

#

Tonio saddled up. There were many pastures on Stirrup and he was headed for the most remote ones, the ones that bordered other ranchos.

CHAPTER 14

Deac finished the breakfast chores after serving Quince a totally unearned meal in his cell. 'Well, I'll try the Sheriff again. He is a busy man, Quince, I been tryin' to catch him to let him know what you were so kind to tell." He grabbed the phone on his desk.

"Sheriff."

"Sheriff this is Deac, you got a minute so's you could come down to the dungeon and talk with my client?"

"Not really. What's up?"

"He wants to tell you all about his drug habit and where he gets the drugs."

"Be right there."

Ben got an ear full and then some.

#

Tonio remounted after checking the brand on the cow he had pushed into the corral and the squeeze chute. Her brand was as botched as the others. "That makes six head with the botched brands. Whoever do this knows nothing of branding or, maybe, is trying to get someone in trouble," he said in Spanish to the horse.

The horse nodded his agreement.

#

Ben returned from the court house with the warrants he needed in hand, unsigned. The Judge was out of town for the weekend. Now it was time to start cracking all this dope dealing in his jurisdiction. He was smiling, until he noticed his boots were dusty.

"Units 2 and 11 meet 1 at the office."

"Unit 2."

"Unit 11."

#

After Chet decided this was a good day for a ride just to relax, he saddled up and rode to the large catch pens where his father died. Two steers were standing in one of the pens. Something about them was wrong, but he couldn't put his finger on the problem.

After riding around the entire complex of pens, he noted, "Fresh truck tracks, a couple days old maybe, coming in from the south and leaving the same way. Eighteen wheelers if my tracking skills are still with me. Wonder what they were up to. I thought I told Billy not to put cows on this pasture for a while." He talked to the wind and received no answers.

Riding off a ways along the tracks he came to a spot where many cows had crossed the tracks. He rode back to the pens.

The two steers he pushed into a small pen used to catch sick stuff or those that bore a look. He dismounted and pushed them through the squeeze one at a time. The first had his brand over a /7 and the second was a Double D under his brand. "Someone is trying to load my ranch with rustled stock. For what reason and who?" he wondered aloud. "What I really don't need right now is the law running all over my ranch."

#

Roy Carson picked up the phone and pushed the buttons. The rings came through the ear piece loud and clear.

"Yeah. Who's this?"

"Hey, Pony Boy, it's me, Roy. Does that invite to some good marijuana still stand. I need to mellow out. My boss is such a jerk and I need the job. How about it?"

There was quiet on the line for a full minute. "Pony, I need some kind of medication. I'm so uptight I can't see straight and if I write another bum story like this last one, I'm out of a job. Please?"

Still the quiet, but no disconnect.

A full thirty seconds later, "Come on over and I'll see what I got. I'm due for a joint anyhow."

"I'll be right there." Ray grabbed his keys thinking, *'He's gonna want me to smoke with him. Ah, so what?'*

#

"Hola."

"Juan, this is Tonio. I need to talk with you now. Right now. This is very serious, mucho malo."

"Where you at?"

"Headed for Witch Well Tavern. Can you meet me there?"

"Si. On my way, hombre, on my way. Be there in 30 minutes." He rushed out only to find the only vehicle he had was his personal vehicle. "No problem, it's my day off. What else could happen?"

#

"I can hardly see the road for the tears, Lord. Keep me safe, please," Aggie cried out as she navigated the car toward St. Johns. "This isn't easy, Lord. I loved that man and You allowed him to die before I could get him down the aisle. I'm not happy about that at all. Someday, You wanna explain all this to me."

She instantly felt comfort and embarrassment. "Who am I to question You?"

Her vision cleared.

#

Roy knocked on the door to a dump. The yard was crap. "Don't you ever pick up anything, Pony Boy? The County dump looks better than this," he said to the door.

He knocked again.

"Just a minute. Who's there?"

"Roy Carson. Let me in."

"Hold your horses. I ain't dressed yet."

"Pony, you knew I was coming. What's up."

No answer.

#

“Apache County Sheriff’s Office, how may I direct your call?” Diane said, calmly. She had only been on the desk for an hour.

“This is Coconino County Sheriff speaking. May I speak to your Sheriff.”

“One minute please.”

Ben picked up the phone and said, “Ben Beazley here.”

“Sheriff, we got a truck south of Flag loaded with dope. Tags are registered to Stirrup Ranch. You working anything in that direction?”

“Yes. I would appreciate any info you might have on that truck. Did you get a driver?”

“No driver. Engine is shot, we believe. Tell ya what. I’ll work up the truck and send you everything we get, signed, sealed, and delivered. I remember the help you gave us on that case last year. So, what ya got going there?”

“Well, it’s a long story of drugs, snipers, and rustlers. The dope part includes a deputy killed. . .

Ben told most of the story.

#

The two deputies stopped and looked the house over before deciding that Tom would take the front door and knock, while Twila Collins went around back. “I’ll give you two clicks on the mike when I’m in place.”

“Works.”

Twila trotted across the road around the bend out of sight from the house, moved through the salt cedars along the river, jumped the Little Colorado, and eased up to the back of the house. She reached up and pushed the send button on her shoulder mike twice. In her ear phone she heard two clicks back. The sound of his car rolling around the corner of Water Street told her Tom was moving to the front door.

She moved in on the back door and crouched out of sight on the door knob side. The wall was unpainted cement block which allowed her to lean into it without the wall creaking and giving her position away.

The sound of a knock on the front door was followed by Tom yelling, “Mariano, I need to speak with you. Come out here.”

The sound of rustling feet from inside the house came in her direction followed by someone opening the door next to her and trying to do it quietly. She grabbed her baton from her belt and waited. A foot stepped out and then another, Mariano, looked back over his shoulder as he tried to shut the door. She swung the baton at his shin bone.

“Wha?” Mariano hit the dirt outside the door.

She jumped on him and rolled him belly down, yelling, “Round back, Tom,” as she planted a knee in the middle of his back.

Mariano said, “Woooooof,” as the air left his lungs.

She pulled first his right arm and then his left arm back and cuffed him just as his wife landed on her back. It was her turn to, “Woooooof,” as the 300 pound woman knocked her off and onto her back. The Ramerez girl bellied down on her just as Tom came through the back door.

“We don’t need her, Twila. Let her go.” Tom was laughing as he put his foot in the middle of Mariano’s back. “Let her go,” he repeated.

“You could help me with this half ton of blubber, you know.”

“I don’t weigh anywhere near that much, puta. Let my husband go.” The Ramerez girl was rolling around for emphasis. Tom reached over with his baton, stuck it in an arm pit, and pushed, rolling the very heavy woman off his partner.

Twila rolled and jumped up, seething. The wife was rolled to her very ample belly and her hands pulled behind her back. “You wanna hand me your cuffs, Tom? We’re taking them both in and then we’ll come back to execute the search warrant.”

It was a very short trip to the jail.

#

"Hey, this is just the stuff I need. I feel mellow, very mellow. For the first time in days I feel like I'm alive. Thanks, Pony Boy."

"How big a load you want?"

"Enough for a week oughta do. I can do some great writing with this in me. My writing will really impress my boss now. I just can't thank you enough for putting me onto this." He took another drag, "Not enough."

"Don't make me sorry for this, Roy. Somehow, this don't seem kosher."

"Why? I'm enjoying myself. Join me."

Pony Boy rolled up a blunt.

#

Aggie stood in the Funeral Parlor, "No, he's not my husband. We were to be married next week. He has no family that I am aware of. His parents are dead. He had no siblings. I have never heard him talk of aunts, uncles, or cousins. So, where do we go from here?"

"Well, I will need a court order to allow you to represent the deceased's family in this matter."

"Somehow, I don't think that will be a problem."

#

Ben arrived at his office just as Mariano was being unloaded from the back seat of unit 11 followed by his wife coming out of unit 2. He got the feeling Twila had something against the lady the way she was handling the heavy Ramerez girl. 'What is her first name, anyhow?' Ben thought.

Out loud he said, "Donia. That's it, Donia."

#

"Thanks, Barto. I needed the nap."

"Wanna buy some good stuff, compadré? Give you a good deal."

"Nah, I know where to get all I want free."

"Tell me."

"Nah. I don't use anymore. It needs to stay hidden."

"You cheat me, man."

"Goodbye, thanks for the flop. Nice couch."

Barto reached out and grabbed Miguel by the shirt front. "I wanna know and I want in on the deal."

A sharp object drew blood from Barto's chin. He looked down. Miguel's butterfly knife practically up his nose caused him to let go.

Miguel went out the door as Barto ran for his gun.

Miguel stopped behind the door and waited. As Barto came through the doorway, his Glock leading the charge, Miguel slammed the door in his face.

The gun went off putting a bullet through the door and Miguel's ribs before it fell from Barto's hand as he fell, unconscious, to the porch. Miguel picked up the Glock and pulled Barto's car keys from the pocket of his baggy shorts before calmly walking to the car with his left hand covering the flow of blood coming from his right side just above his belt. "Hurts like hell. This is not a good thing."

He started the car and, as he left, noticed Barto still laid out in the doorway. "He ain't gonna be happy with me."

Miguel circled as close to the location of his rifle as possible, jumped out, ran, grabbed the gun, and ran back. He threw rocks all over the place as he peeled out for Holbrook.

#

"Mariano," Ben began, "if you help me, I'll help you. The grass found on you is from the same stuff dropped the night Deputy Billings was killed. You are implicated and may be charged with a piece of killing a deputy, my deputy. That could mean the gas chamber for you and a long time in jail for Donia. You don't want that, do you?"

"I didn't kill, Oscar. He was a good man. I just smoke pot."

"Who is your supplier?"

"Ross."

"How do you make the buy?'

"I call him. If I tell you everything, will you let us go."

"I can't make deals, you know that, but I can influence the County Attorney and the court."

"Yeah." Mariano stopped talking and began thinking. Finally, he said, "I cooperate."

#

Aggie rolled into town and, knowing the Judge would be at Maria's for lunch, decided to talk with him there. The place was closed. No sign in the window or lights on inside. She drove on to Maria's to find out what was wrong with her friend.

Maria answered the door after the second knock, tears fresh on her cheeks.

"What's wrong?"

"He is the one. My Miguel is the shooter. I have found the bullets."

"He killed my Billy? But, that's not possible. Billy always gave him work and tried to help him any way he could. Not Miguel."

The two women hugged as Maria cried, "Thinking back, I think it is him."

"I'll kill him. He killed my Billy." Aggie backed away from Maria, "Where is he?"

"I don't know. He has not been home for a long time. You cannot kill him. I must go to Ben and tell him. He will deal with my son and not you."

They stood facing each other. Anger, hurt, mourning, pain as deep as it gets ravished each of the women. They had been friends forever and now this. One had lost a son, a lover, and the other had lost the love of her life.

Both of them leaned in and hugged, sobbing huge tears on each other's shoulder. They cried. They rocked. They suffered until, as if by verbal agreement, they parted. Maria went to the kitchen and put on the coffee pot. Angie started getting the cups and condiments from the cupboard. Within minutes they were sipping and chomping on some day old tortillas while sitting on opposite sides of the table.

"What do we do now?" Maria asked.

"Call Ben. He's the law. Only he has the right to deal with this." Aggie did not want to say that or feel that or live that, she wanted to kill Miguel herself for the pain he caused her and this woman who was her friend, but because she was her friend, she knew what was right and was willing to let the law deal with the son.

"How long has Chet promised to marry you?"

"Since high school. We first made love down by the river on a blanket under a beautiful night sky as he whispered love words in my ear. I believed him. Miguel never did after he was sixteen and found out through the rumor mill in town. One of my friends let slip that Miguel's father was Chet. He almost tore the house apart in his anger. Chet had refused him a summer job that spring and Billy put him to work way out from the house laying pipe for new drinkers. I knew he hated Chet, but never did the thought come that he would try to kill him."

"He may kill him now after he killed Billy. He has nothing to lose now. Call Ben."

Maria dialed the number.

#

"I will kill Chet after I make sure everyone knows that he is dealing drugs. I will let the Sheriff arrest him and then he will die." Miguel moved the car into the exit lane for Holbrook and a phone.

#

The Witch Well Tavern was a dead joint as Tonio pulled in. Nobody was in the place except a chubby man behind the bar with a wide smile and a three day beard. "What'll it be, cowboy?"

"Just a Coke, por favor," Tonio replied.

The bartender walked to the cooler doors, opened one, and pulled a Coke from a partially used six pack. Tonio watched and saw the deer carcass hanging in the side room aging.

The bartender sat the Coke on the bar, "Four bits, fifty cents, one half of a dollar, cheap at half the price, whatever that means. How's the cow punching coming along?"

Tonio popped the top and took a long drink of sugar and caffeine. "It's pretty good. I like the job and the cows like me." He watched Juan's car pull into the parking lot.

"Wow. Looks like a party getting started. You expecting company?"

"Si. It is my cousin, Juan."

"Your cousin is a deputy?"

"Si."

Juan strolled to the front door, hesitated, looked around before pulling the door open, and entered the bar. Seeing Tonio at the bar he climbed a stool next to him and ordered, "I'll have what he's having."

"Oh, a couple of really big spenders out for a wild afternoon, I can tell."

"Yup, that's us." Juan said, popping the top of the can placed in front of him. He, too, saw the deer carcass.

Juan looked the bartender in the eye, "You know, Cliff, it ain't deer season."

"Yeah, I know, Deputy. You gonna bust me for rescuing a deer hit by a car and having two busted legs. Feller brought it in last night after hitting it four miles east of here."

"I'm gonna buy that story this time, but Game and Fish come through and they could confiscate this whole place and put you away, you know."

Cliff looked around before adding, "Here I am, twenty five miles from anywhere and the only building in sight, no electric but what I make with the generator, no phone, no radio since the one the Sheriff gave me smoked, and the way this place is a jumping on Sundays when the bars in New Mexico are closed and the folks from the Zuni reservation roll in, the problems with the casual travelers out here, and you want me to worry about a deer carcass?

"If I had phone service I could call those things in and all, but without the service, well, you know. Game and Fish usually has a blind eye on me, anyhow."

Juan dropped the subject and looked at Tonio, "Que pasa?"

"Let's go outside," Tonio replied.

"Look, you two stay right here and I'll go outside. Gotta use the outhouse anyhow." Cliff walked out the back way.

Tonio began talking.

#

Ben looked at the two prisoners, "So, let me get this straight. You buy from Ross by calling him or meeting him at the Concho Bar on Thursdays. The rustlers call you on the phone to get the actions started and pay you with cash that comes to your post office box and you have no idea who sets it up. Donia has nothing to do with any of it except spend the money. Is that the sum of it?"

"Yes, Sheriff," they both said, nodding their heads.

"Okay, I'll get someone to take your statements and you can sign them. Court will set your bail Monday." Ben led them to the cell block and had Deac tuck them in separate cells. There was no isolation for women in the jail. Deac hung a blanket through the bars and said, "If you need privacy, just hang this over the bars," and handed her a dozen clothespins.

#

Aggie remembered what she came to the café for and called the Judge's office. No answer. Then she remembered it was Saturday and called his home. No answer. She left a message on the answering machine knowing he rarely stayed home on the weekends. His joy was fishing and this was prime fishing weather.

Chapter 15

Ben sat in his office thinking about all that was going on. Two rustlers in the jail, two users squealing on suppliers, a shooter identified, a truck found, another in New Mexico, cows with botched brands, cows disappearing . . . His phone rang.

"Sheriff."

"Sheriff, there is a man on the phone who won't give his name, won't talk to me, and says there's a dead man in a shack just off the Rez in Sanders."

"I'll take it."

He waited for the phone lines to click and said, "Sheriff, how can I help you."

"This man is dead."

"Who, and where are you?"

"Barto is dead. He has blood from his nose. I am at my house. Barto is at his house in Sanders along the road to Gallup." He hung up.

"Hey, wait," Ben yelled at the phone which buzzed in his ear.

He walked out of the office and into dispatch. Did you get a caller ID on that call?"

"You've got to be kidding. You know that is not an option up there."

"Just checking. Who's on in Sanders this fine and lovely day?"

"Unit 12 – Will Conner."

"Sic him on this one and roll the ME. Will knows Sanders like no one else on the squad. He can find the house of Barto somewhere in Sanders along the road to Gallup. If I remember rightly, Barto is one of our suspected dealers in that area."

"I'll get him on it and I think you're right on Barto."

"Just what I needed was another dead man."

"Job security, Boss, job security."

The phone rang.

"Sheriff's Office, how may I help you."

She listened for a moment.

"One moment please."

"It's for you. Some nut case wants to report a very large stash of dope."

"What kind of a crazy day we got here? I'll take it in my office."

He walked to his desk, sat in the chair, picked up the phone, punched the line button, and said, "Sheriff Beazley here, how may I help you."

"Sheriff Ben, this is Miguel. I can tell you who is doing the major drug smuggling in your jurisdiction."

"Miguel, you need to turn yourself in. Billy died and you're tagged for it."

"Shut up and listen. I will never turn myself in. The hombre' you want is Chet Handley, mi padre. He has a shed beyond the corrals at the main house loaded with weed and speed and probably more. I will leave a map on the milepost sign just south of the turnoff to the headquarters. Good hunting."

"Miguel, I will follow up on this. Come in and let's talk."

"No. You will have to kill me to catch me." He hung up.

Ben sat back in his chair with the phone still in his hand. "Damn. Damn. Damn."

"Diane," he shouted through the open doorway. "Is there anything going right this afternoon?"

"Not that I know of, Boss."

Juan walked through the door in civvies and sat in his usual chair.

"What do you want, Deputy Vasquez?"

"Ten minutes."

"Go."

Juan shared with him the information he had gotten from Tonio, making sure to leave out Tonio's name.

"Who told you all this?"

"Won't say. I went out and looked at two head myself."

"Where?"

"Stirrup corrals."

"Which one?"

"Not sayin'." Juan looked Ben in the eyes and added, "My source is my source. That person will not be named in any report or even courtroom testimony. I will go to jail for Contempt and still not say the name."

Ben remembered some family ties in Juan's life. "Okay. Fair enough."

The two of them sat and looked at each other. Ben pulled out a cigar and lit up. Juan looked at the procedure and said, "Where's mine?"

"Over to Lenny's or at the store."

"Buy ya a beer?"

"Never thought you'd ask." Ben got out of the chair, walked through the doorway, and yelled at Diane, "I'll be in my other office." He stopped.

Juan got up and followed.

Ben said to Diane, "Tell everyone to go to normal patrol mode. Drop all investigations where they are if possible and take the rest of the weekend for a rest. And, please call Maria and Aggie for me, they're both at Maria's, and ask them to please stop by the other office for a face to face in about an hour."

"Sure, Ben, the rest of the weekend, whoopee, tomorrow's Monday. But, don't worry, I'll send the whole crowd to you down there, Lenny can use the business. Hope he doesn't run out of soda or coffee."

"He won't," said Juan as he followed his hero's back down the hall.

#

"What's your thoughts, John."

"How would I know, Chet. You're the boss. I just get beat up, shot, and run errands."

"Let's get some dinner and think on this."

#

Bud looked down at his wife and remembered again the first time he saw her. She was sliding down the slide at Pioneer School. Her skirt flew up in her face and exposed the shorts she had on underneath. He laughed at her for wearing shorts and a skirt.

She said, "You laugh, but it keeps twerpy boys with cooties like you from looking up a lady's dress when she's on the slide."

It was third grade.

The next day she had kicked him and he knew it was love. He still had the scar on his shin to prove it.

"What are you thinking, Bud?"

"Remembering."

"Remembering what?"

"You on a slide, shorts, a kick in the shin, and a bunch other events that told me you were the gal for me, forever."

"I never kicked you! That must have been one of your other girlfriends. Maybe that Ramerez gal, what was her name?"

"I wouldn't be able to remember, even if you put me to torture. Once you were in my life, no other gal had a chance to even attract a look." A nurse walked by and his head turned.

"Oh, I can see that."

He laughed. "I did that on purpose so I could see your smile come back."

"I'm ready to blow this joint, husband of mine. Let's go home."

"Doctor will be by shortly. You can talk to him. This isn't a simple cut and run surgery you went through. It's hard on the body. We'll wait on the doctor."

"This bed is hard on the body. We'll wait."

He laughed again.

She smiled.

#

Lenny walked to the door and flipped the switches to the outside lights on his place just as Maria and Aggie arrived. He pointed to the back corner table where Ben and Juan were sitting with Deac, who had just gotten off work and decided it was a good time for a beer, root beer.

The two ladies walked to the table. Ben saw them first and stood, taking off his hat. Juan and Deac stood, and reached for chairs to assist the ladies.

"Well, aren't we just the most cavalier men in the state. Hat's off and chairs assisted, that strikes me as buttering up a couple of the ladies of the community," Aggie's sharp tongue carved up the air.

Juan said, "Aggie, you never let a man be a real man without jabbing him, do you?"

"Juan, you are always a gentleman, but Ben is finally learning. You must be rubbing off on him, and that's a good thing. I just wanted him to know that I saw the effort."

"Don't expect it again, Aggie. You can park yourself and join the conversation anytime you'd like. We'll treat ya just like one of the boys. It's your turn to buy cuz you're three minutes late."

"I'll buy," said Maria. "I was the one that caused us to be late. Had to put on my face, you know."

Everyone chuckled at that. For a woman over 40, Maria was a good looking woman by anyone's standards. Aggie was no slouch, either. They both drew attention wherever they went.

"So, Ben, what's this all about?"

He told her all he wanted to tell her and said, "We have so much info at the present time that we need to regroup, rethink, and react, and get to the point we are one step ahead of the perps. Somehow I know, not think, know, that they are all tied together. If the Governor had sent us the man we asked for, we'd be closer to the answers.

"So, bottom line. I sent my men to bed, except for routine patrols and such. Left a message for the Judge that said I needed him as soon as he gets back from whatever lake he's haunting this weekend. I'll get the warrants and we'll go check things out in an organized manner so all the ducks are in a row, the t's crossed, and the i's dotted, when it comes time for arrests and trial.

"Are you with me?" Ben concluded.

Everyone said yes or nodded, and reached for their drink which Lenny was just delivering.

"No one talks to anyone about this without my go ahead. Understood?"

Again the affirmative answers.

#

"Truck is here."

"Meet you at the shed."

#

"Well, young lady, you may go home if you promise to stay in bed for at least two more days, except when nature calls, you will take your medicine like a good girl, and you will call me if anything feels or looks or smells wrong."

"I can do that, Doctor."

"I will make sure of that, Doctor."

"Get dressed slow and easy, pack your bag, and wait for the nurse to drive you to the door."

"I can get that, Doctor."

"Nope. House rules. I can't put someone in your jail, you can't roll someone out of my hospital. Deal?"

"Deal."

An hour later Carrie was in the front seat of the van, after a long climb up, and headed for her home and her flock.

#

The truck rolled off Stirrup by using back roads and some faint two rut roads. It wouldn't stop or be stopped until it reached Amarillo, Texas.

"Chet, you need to come look at this."

"What? I'm whipped."

"Footprints behind the shed. They come from over the hill and return the same way. Looks like the shooter's prints. Back wall has been messed with, also."

"What do you think," he said, looking down when the flashlight in John's hand shined.

"If I were boss, we'd be moving this stuff quickly, as in right now, and taking the shed completely away after cleaning up the dirt under that product."

"Let's get on with it."

The two of them tore down the building after loading all the weed and speed in a stake bed truck and driving it to an old line shack two miles away, about a mile north of Homestead Well. Chet was dragging as John threw the last light pieces of metal from the building into the stake bed truck.

Chet said, "Don't pull your gut, we don't have time for the hospital."

"I like watching you work. It's a nice change, boss."

"You drive. I'll rest."

The truck rolled again, loaded with evidence that would get both of them a death sentence or at the least life inside the toughest prison in the state. Chet off loaded all the metal and junk from the shed into a hole downwind of the house that was there for disposing trash. On still days, gas would be poured on the pile in the bottom and lighted. It was moldering with tiny wisps of smoke and smell from the fire started three days ago. The corpse of the dead cow did not help the smell a bit. Every couple years they had dug a new hole to replace the full hole, for as far back as Chet could remember.

Chet ran the Case front loader/back hoe to fill in this hole and then to dig a new one twenty feet to the South while John went back to the shed site and poured gasoline and old motor oil over the entire plot of land, twelve feet by 10 feet. When he threw the match on the ground it went up with a whoosh and heat that drove him back. The ground burned. Every leaf or seed of pot, burned. It all burned. John grabbed green juniper branches and threw them on the fire. The sweet odor of burning juniper filled the air.

#

Lary Handley and Crackers had heard the truck lumbering along the dirt road west to north as they prepared to do some more nighttime exploring. Lary had his camouflage on and the dog was wearing his working collar. "Crackers, we might just want to go that way first and see what's so important they are running a truck at this time of night."

Crackers thumped his tail on the cabin floor.

Lary grabbed night vision goggles and opened the front door, "Let's go get'em, whatever it is."

#

Miguel had watched the building being hauled away. He watched the backhoe work from his favorite perch on a hillock two hundred yards from the Stirrup house and only fifty yards or so from the shed. He watched the truck roll to the old line cabin. He had worked there for Billy.

The thought of Billy dead had hit him hard when the news came over the radio as he traveled on back roads from Holbrook to the ranch. It was so bad; he had stopped the car and prayed for Billy's soul like he was taught to do by the nuns. After the prayer, he wiped his eyes and swore even greater vengeance on Stirrup and his father.

All that was going on down below him was plain and open to him. He knew they had discovered his tracks. They would know what was coming now. He knew they were in a tight spot with the botched brands in the corrals and on the pastures. They were the ones responsible. If Chet had treated him like a son, he would have told them how to beat it all now. Of course, the shooter would have been out of the picture, the botched brands would have been out of the picture, and the rustling would have been out of the picture. Miguel could not remember how many head he had caused to be rebranded sloppily and dumped on Stirrup land. He had also made more than enough money to pay all the folks that did the work and took the risks.

"All of that will stop once I am dead. No one will know for sure I did it. No one will care because it will all stop. Ben will try to figure it out, but there is no way," Miguel said to nothing. He just said it out loud to hear something other than the night noises and the digging.

He cried again, "The only regret is you, Billy. Why did you have to come after me, you loveable old fool? Why is it you were not my father?"

That he had hurt his mother never even crossed his mind.

The whoosh of the shed site going up in flames caught his attention. He jumped. The light was so bright he was sure John could see him. Moments later he was backing off and swore he could feel the heat from the fire.

"Time to move," he whispered. He slung the 7 MM on his shoulder and walked. His ribs were grinding together even after he had bound them with a torn tee shirt and some web strapping he found in the trunk of the car.

#

As the fire burned down, Chet scooped the embers with the front loader and dumped them in the new hole. He kept it up until all the ash, embers, and charcoal was in the hole.

John said, "You gonna fill this in with dirt from the hole?"

"No. I'm going to make that the new hole and put the dirt from it to cover this ash and hide the hole the ash is in. How's that sound?"

"Little more travel back and forth, but sounds great."

The two of them worked their way closer as Miguel watched, Chet and John were oblivious as they continue what they thought was an exercise of hiding all the evidence.

John said loud enough for all to here, "That about does it. Nobody going to find nothing here."

Miguel chuckled under his breath, "You may not think so, Johnnie Boy, but I will attempt to make sure you are wrong."

Two hours later, the job was done and two of them climbed in the two vehicles and headed for the house.

#

Crackers was alerting in three directions. He gave a man alert in one direction and a drug alert in two others. Lary was not interested in the man alert. He knew the dog would let him know if the man started in their direction. He was very interested in the drugs.

Lary pointed and said, "Alert, find."

The dog took off in a slow trot that allowed Lary to keep up. The sage and junipers kept them zigging and zagging enough that their travel distance was doubled. 'Too bad there isn't a nice straight road here,' Lary said to the dog.

The dog changed course a little and within a hundred yards they were jogging down a two rut road that had just recently been used for the first time in a long time. It had been used in two directions from the looks of it. Same tire tread both times. Tracks in this country lasted a long time, if it did not rain and the wind was not too bad. Even in the wind, sheltered spots of dirt would still tell the story.

A half mile later they came to the line shack. The door was not locked. They walked in and pushed the button on a flashlight.

"Ooooooweeee, Crackers, we have found the mother lode. There has to be at least a few million dollars' worth of dope in this shack." He took a couple of pictures with a small cube flash camera.

"Let's go see what that other alert was all about, Crackers."

"Alert, find." They were off again, this time following the road in the other direction.

The smell of smoke stopped them as the lights of Stirrup came in sight. The sound of a tractor filled the air. Two men could be seen working in the light given from two sets of headlights.

Lary took a couple of pictures without the flash on the wild chance that something might be seen when they were developed. He and the dog snuggled deep into the sparse grass behind a large clump of sage.

#

Ben attempted to sleep, but the facts he knew on all that was going on rattled around in his head like marbles in a pickup bed on a bad road and were not coming together in a clear picture. The shooter, Billy's death, rustling, Oscar's death, and drugs just did not make for an easy puzzle. How many crooks would it take to make all this happen? What kind of equipment? Where could an outfit stash all this between uses? What's the drugs got to do with the shooting and the rustling?

He got up and took two aspirin to knock the headache that much thinking caused, either the thinking or the five or six beers.

#

Miguel watched as they drove the two vehicles back to the ranch house and got out. He couldn't hear what they said, but there was a discussion. As the two men started for the back door, Miguel put a round in the dirt between them and the door, calmly got up, and walked away, holding his side as he walked.

#

Lary was watching as the shot rang out and the dust flew in front of the retiring men. He stayed low, hoping the shooter did not have him pegged. He put Crackers behind him and the dog didn't mind at all. The dark image of a man seemed to float across dark night in the sage way off to his left. "Is that the shooter, Crackers, is that him?"

Down below was a comedy routine free for the watching, as Lary saw the two men dancing and shuffling trying to find cover, get in the house, shut off the lights, and otherwise spinning around like a pair of tops. John was the first to hit the dirt behind the truck.

Chet made the door. It was locked. He grabbed for the keys. He dropped them. He ran around the corner of the house into the safety of darkness.

By the time either head came up again down at the ranch house, Lary and Crackers decided to head for the cabin and go to sleep. "Tomorrow," Lary said, "We will call in reinforcements."

#

Lew and Sue sat in the kitchen, coffee in hand, and smiled at each other across the table.

Sue took a sip of coffee and, "I haven't felt like this in years. I love you, Lew. I have not been the wife I should have been for a few years now, but I am going to be that wife from now on."

"You've been everything to me. Don't go putting yourself down. I love you so much, you couldn't drive me away."

#

Bud sat in the bedroom, drinking another cup of coffee, as he watched Carrie sleep. She whimpered a bit now and then. A loud exclamation from her at 6 AM had lifted him right out of bed and over to the closet where his gun was. He felt like a fool when he realized what had awakened him and decided since he was awake he'd work on a special breakfast for the family. The kids would be waking up and they were always hungry, the boys especially. Those kids of his were known to eliminate two gallons of milk, four boxes of cereal, and a couple of loaves of bread made into french toast which meant at least 18 eggs. His deputy pay was just adequate, only because he or Carrie would not allow them to eat that much except on very special occasions.

Within minutes, the two youngest were on his lap discussing Mama's surgery.

"You mean no more kids, Dad?"

"Yes, son."

"But, Dad, Mother wanted at least two more, she told me so."

"Yes, Honey, I know, but God decided differently, I guess."

The eldest girl still at home walked in, "How's Mom?"

"She's okay. It will take a while, but you won't have to carry the load too long. She'll be up and about in six or eight weeks."

"But, Dad. I won't be able to go to the softball camp if I have to do that." She stopped short. "I will do it for you and Mom. I won't be selfish."

The oldest boy stuck his head around the corner, "That will be a nice change."

Within moments, the kitchen was filled with kids and Dad. Each kid with his or her own questions and comments piling one over the other in volume until Carrie, hunched over and holding her pillow to her stomach, came staggering through the door. "What's all this noise? Can't a girl get some rest around here?"

The kids all jumped for her, but Bud was faster. He jumped between Carrie and the flock, "Whoa, kids. Mom can't be trampled for a couple of weeks, yet. One at a time, youngest first, short easy hug and a smooch, then back off."

Carrie hugged each one in turn and gave them a kiss. "I want to go to the church this morning."

"But, the doctor told you to stay in bed for two days, honey, and that was yesterday. Remember?"

#

The town was quiet, way too quiet in Ben's opinion. All he could think of, as he sat on his porch polishing his boots, were the problems. Having no family, he sat alone much of the time.

Juan was returning home and saw Ben. He slowed the car and turned into the dirt patch that was Ben's front yard and parking lot. "Hey, boss, I don't have much time. Gotta go on duty."

"Have a seat, Juan. Gimme your boots and I'll polish them for you. Isn't that what Marines do in their spare time?"

"No, I think you use that for a time to think."

"What's on your mind?"

"I been thinkin', and it hurts. The shooter, the brands, rustling, deaths just don't make sense. There's a factor here that is missing. I think I figured out what it is."

"And?"

"I think we got two rustlers, one of which is the shooter. The shooter is out to finish Stirrup for some reason. The other rustler is money hungry and is probably the drug side of the story. The shooter took out Billy because Billy knew something he didn't want told, and the dopers took out Oscar, or at least were the cause." He stopped and stared at the Sheriff who was sitting there with his mouth open.

Ben said, "Could be. I think you got the shootings right, but not the drugs and the rustling. I wonder which of us is right?"

"We'll just have to find out, Boss. I gotta go. If I'm late my boss will cut my pay."

"Nah, you're on the clock now." Ben smiled. "You've come a long way in the last week or so, I'm proud to have you on the force. But, don't ruin any more vehicles, okay?

"Yeah, boss. I'm off."

"By the way, Miguel is the shooter."

#

Aggie awoke on Maria's couch.

Maria was bustling in the kitchen mumbling under her breath as Aggie walked in. "How you feeling this morning, Maria?"

"Very good. Mi nino did not come home. I do not think I will see him alive ever again. I have prayed to Mary that she will protect him, but for what, to die in a prison?"

"I don't think he will make prison, Maria. He will die fighting before he will go to prison. He is a man who will never surrender, I think."

"He is a boy. A boy who has been hurt by the father he never had and is striking out in enfado, anger. This man use me for years, it take me this many to learn that, por que?"

"We women have our dreams and are willing to wait for the fulfillment. I waited for Billy as you have waited for Chet." The tears ran down her cheeks as she saw the tears in Maria's eyes. "We must deal with our disappointment, our sorrow, and get on with life, even though I'm not sure I want to right now."

"Me, also. I will go to the church to pray and light a candle."

"I think I will go to work. Maybe in work I can bury my hurt. I need the Judge, anyhow. Be blessed, my friend."

"And you, Amiga."

#

Deac Washburn arrived at the jail on time at 8 AM carrying his homework and books for his course work. Diane and Lane were changing the guard in the dispatch room as he slid past trying not to be seen.

Diane said, "Deac, I thought you were gonna be a deputy instead of that wimpy computer stuff."

"You may laugh, young lady, but I just might do both. How about if I design a computer program that will solve crimes? What would you say to that?"

"How's about one that prevents crimes," Lane chimed in.

"Hmmm, hadn't thought it through that much. Prevent crimes. Nah, then the deputy wouldn't have anything to do. I'd lose my job and so would you both. We wouldn't want that to happen, would we?"

"Nope. I like to eat."

"Me, too."

Deac continued his journey to the jailer's hole. As he sat his books on the desk, he heard Diane say, "Good morning and good night."

"Sleep tight," said Lane.

"Yeah, right. With my two kids? Ain't gonna happen. We're goin' to the pool. I can sleep there while the lifeguard watches. They know my routine."

Deac laughed, "Wonder when I'll find a wife and all the trimmings?"

#

Maria entered the old adobe Chapel of San Juan, dipped her fingers in the holy water, and made the sign of the cross, before moving deeper into the Sanctuary of her beliefs. Arriving at the front row of pews, she genuflected before turning to the alcove where many candles already burned on the altar. She put a bill in the box, took the taper, lit it, lit a candle on the altar, and kneeled to pray. Her fingers were still wet from the Holy Water at the door and left a spot on the front of her blouse as she put her hands over her heart, and wept her prayer.

She was so intent on her own sorrow and focused on the God she loved that Carrie's hand on her shoulder startled her. "May I join you?"

"Oh! Please do."

Carrie put her arm around Maria as she slowly kneeled with the help of Bud.

The tears of the two women fell to the kneeler as Bud went through the ritual of lighting a candle, three candles. He had been told that in the eastern culture of Jesus' days, to say something three times was a contract. Bud was making a contract with God. Peace for peace. Comfort for comfort. Trust for trust. Love for love. All he really wanted was his wife's happiness.

#

Lary and Crackers climbed into the old truck and headed for town. On the seat between them was a backpack full of samples from the stash they had found during the night. He had his custom built Kimber .45 automatic in a holster under his left arm, 2 spare magazines were under his right arm. A long hard case with an unlatched lid lay on the floorboard on the passenger side. Inside that case was an M-16 with the selector switch in the three round burst position.

Crackers knew what all the gun oil smell meant.

Chapter 16

The clock on the wall said tick tick tick tick as the hands indicated it was 8:30. Under the clock, the door opened as deputies filed in one at a time and headed for the table along the wall where the coffee, juice, and bear sign were located. Some grabbed a Styrofoam cup and others held their own personal mug, most of the personals were grungy from much use and no washing.

Juan was the first one there. He filled his cup and waited to sit beside Shef in the back of the room. The two rookies liked to be out of the firing line when the heavy discussions went down.

Juan said, “Whatcha think?”

“I think I will just keep quiet unless called upon. It worked in the Army, it oughta work here.”

“Sounds like a plan.”

At 8:15 Ben walked in followed by Deac.

“Get what you need and get set, it will be a long session, maybe.” Ben yelled.

Deac filled his grungy mug and grabbed a donut before sitting at the seat nearest the door.

“Okay, first up. Lew, anything new on the tracks?”

“No, Sir.”

“Juan, what ya got on the key?”

“Found the box. Registered to a Harley Davidson. Address does not exist. USPS Postmaster states there were only a few pieces of mail to that box, all addressed to Harley Davidson. She had no idea who the man was. No one recalls him getting the box, which was dated three months ago. End of the line right there."

"Rustlers – We have Quince, he fingered a dealer and the other rider, Mariano Alverez. One dead body from the truck wreck identified as a petty crook with a record quite short named Edgar Ormstat. If no one claims the body, the county will have to bury him."

A knock sounded at the door.

Lane stuck her head in, "Man here says it's very important that he see you right now."

"Stand easy, men. I'll be right back."

Ben walked out the door to find Lary waiting for him.

"What do you want? I got things to do and you need to deal with your land issues in the court."

"Isn't a land issue, Sheriff." He flipped a badge case open and stuck it up where Ben could see it.

"Arizona Department of Public Safety? The Governor sent you?"

"Who better? I own land here and as it turns out, I'm close to all the problems."

"I have a briefing going with my troops right now, can we talk later?"

"Don't you want to hear what I have for you? I know who the drug kingpin is. I can tell you who the man is that is his sidekick. I also know who the rustler is, I think."

"Come on in. You need to be a part of this meeting."

#

Aggie went into her office carrying a cup of tea after a visit to the employee lounge in the courthouse. In her purse was Billy's .45 Peacemaker. She surmised it just might come in handy should certain people come by with ill intent.

It was a quiet morning. Many of the normally rowdy ones were not in yet. They were at least ten minutes late, but the Judge had not yet arrived, either. An envelope from the Sheriff was on her desk with a note.

She read it. “Please get these signed for me. If the judge has any questions, let me know and I’ll come right over. I think we can wrap this mess up quickly once I have these. Thanks, Ben”

At nine, the Judge still was not in his office.

#

Ben called on Will to give a report on the dead man in Sanders.

“Well, Sheriff, the dead man goes by many names, but the usual was Barto Sergeant. He’s a two bit drug dealer with a reputation of breaking legs for late payment fees. According to his girlfriend, the gun he had in the house was not there. I made an assumption that the gun that did the deed was that gun. Turns out I was right. A hundred yards down the road the gun was found in the bar ditch empty, slide locked back, and no magazine. Fingerprints on the gun match the ones we have on file for Miguel, our shooter. Those prints need to be verified by the state lab before they can be considered a match, but by my very calibrated eyeball, they match.”

He got a chuckle out of that one.

“Walking the dirt road from Barto’s abode to the pavement a bit over two miles away, I found a set of tracks that stepped out of a car, walked out into the sage to a bush with a rag laying over the top of it, turned around, and went back. At the turn around point was the print of a rifle in the sand which appeared to be scoped. Could be Miguel had stashed his 7 MM there and stopped to pick it up. Oh, yeah. I almost forgot. The gun was not the instrument of death. Barto’s nose bone had been hit so hard it pushed into his brain. Death was instantaneous. The gun had recently been fired. Our shooter may have been wounded. There was a spotty trail of blood from the front of the house, if you wanna call it that, to where the car had been parked.”

#

“Juan. Tell what you got on the brands.”

“Not much to tell. Stirrup brand over multiple rustled brands. A couple dozen head found without looking too hard.”

#

“Anybody got anything else?”

Deac raised his hand.

"Yeah, Deac."

"I can make a connection and do a buy if you want. Only you know I am a part of all this or have been involved in the Sheriff's Department, even. Many folks think all us Colored Folk use dem drugs to kill the pain of being so cursed, or some such crap. Just tell me to go."

"Thanks for the offer, but I don't think we'll have to play on your uniqueness that way."

"Uniqueness? I like that."

#

"I'll bring this to a close if no one has anything more."

Ben waited. Nothing.

"Okay. We have two dealers dealing the same drugs Oscar died over. One is in a cell. The other is at large. Both of them probably get their drugs from a local distributor. We have a warrant waiting at the judge's office to deal with that person.

"We will be receiving various warrants as soon as they are signed. Today is the day of reckoning in this county. Before it is over, we will have every crime covered and solved. I hope we will all be in one piece at the end.

"Any questions?"

There were none so Ben ended with, "Remember, keep routine on channel 2 so all the scanners will be happy, but monitor channel 5 for action. Now we wait for the warrants. I want nothing to happen that will ruin the case when this gets to court. You got that."

They all agreed.

#

The truck came around the corner faster than normal as Chet looked out the window of the barn. John pulled the truck into the yard, slammed on the brakes throwing the truck into a slide until it stopped, jumped out, and ran for the house.

"John. Over here," Chet yelled.

John changed directions and slowed down.

Chet waited until he was close and said, "What's the hurry?"

"Line shack was busted into. Some of the bundles were opened. From the pieces on the floor, I think someone took samples and that someone was that damned friend of ours, Lary. Tracks there of a dog, also."

"Damned is right. Let's go put an end to his snooping around with that damned dog. Never did like that dog."

After grabbing a couple of rifles, the two of them climbed in the four wheel drive truck and headed for Homestead Well, through the ranch. On the way one of the riders flagged them down.

"What you want for me to do today, Patron? Without Señor Billy, I have nada." Tonio was startled by the weapons across their laps.

"Just check the water and that ought to do it for today. That drinker over to the west was jammed yesterday, water everywhere. I think I fixed it, but you check and then take off for a couple of days. See ya next week, Tonio. Come to the main house on Monday."

"Si, Patron. I will do as you say." He rode away confused. There were no cows in that pasture and that drinker was not in use. But, he decided to do as he was told and check it. Maybe, just maybe, they had moved cows to that section since he was last there.

John eased out of the truck, raised the rifle in his hands, and took Tonio out of the saddle.

"What did you do that for? He knows nothing."

"He knows there are no cows in that pasture and he knows you just lied to him."

"Let's get that good neighbor of ours. We can bury them both in the same hole."

#

The judge entered his office at 11 AM. His face and arms were bright red and he was struggling to walk.

"What happened to you?"

"Truck broke down fifteen miles from the pavement and I had to walk out. Started walking at 4 yesterday afternoon. My hat blew off and this old body is no longer in shape for a long walk. Got picked up an hour ago. My everything aches."

"Have a seat. I have a bunch of warrants and such for you to sign. The County Attorney has three cases for you to hear today."

"Okay, Aggie, are they valid, properly prepared warrants?"

She looked at him with a grin, "Yes, Sir. Every one of them is. With these Ben will be in position to end the mess going on in this county, from the shooter to the drugs, from the rustling to the murders."

"Hand me a pen, I like the sound of that."

He bent and started signing, glancing at each one. "What's this on Miguel? I would have never guessed. Are they sure?"

"About as sure as possible. His mother turned him in after finding stuff in his closet. She is devastated."

"So, how's Billy?"

Aggie started crying.

"What's wrong?"

"He died on me. Miguel was the one that shot him."

"I am so sorry." He put his arm gently around the shoulders of the sobbing woman.

"I need you to sign this so I can take care of the funeral home for Billy."

He scribbled one more signature. "There. Is that all?"

"For now. What about the County Attorney?"

"What gives there?"

"Drugs."

"Call them and ask that they bring that up at 9 tomorrow morning, please, and then get out of here for a few days. I'll borrow a gal from the County Attorney's Office. I am going to arrange for my truck to get picked up and taken to the shop, and then go home and go to bed after a nice hot shower." He shuffled into his office and grabbed the phone before closing the door.

Aggie ran for the Sheriff's Office, the tears running down her cheeks.

#

Miguel had watched from his hilltop perch as his cousin was shot in the back and fell face first. He waited until the truck was as far away from cover as possible and opened up on the two men in the cab. The difference was, this time he was trying to kill.

The first round hit the front wheel of the accelerating truck almost dead center. The slug found its way into the wheel bearing and jammed the axle to a dead stop. The truck swerved and rolled. Chet was thrown from the truck and John stayed inside due to his seat belt locking up on him. The truck came to rest on its driver's side with the underside facing the shooter. Both men were still conscious.

John called, "You okay?"

"Yeah, I think. My left arm hurts like blazes, but everything else appears to be in working order. Get the rifles. How you doin'?"

"Little blood from my gut, but there's a compression bandage in the glove compartment. Never had a blowout do all that before."

A round came through the floorboards on the driver's side and missed John by no more than two inches.

"That was not a blowout, John. Our little friend is back. Let's take him."

John kicked out the windshield so he could get out without exposing himself to the shooter. He knew only too well how good the shooter's aim was. Wrapping the bandage around his middle as tight as he could stand it, was no fun, but it had to be done. The spare box of ammo went in his cargo pocket. With the rifles in hand, he stepped out of the disabled truck and took cover behind the engine.

"Where you at, Chet?"

Chet waved a hand and said, "Over here," with just enough volume to carry as far as the truck.

John saw the hand not more than thirty feet from his position. "Where's the shooter?"

"Beats me. And, I am not sticking my head up to find out. I think he is out for blood now."

John went to the back of the truck, which was closer to Chet, and said, "I will draw his fire. He has a bolt action rifle so you will have maybe two seconds to get here from there when he fires. You game?"

"Let's do it. I can't do anything from here."

"Here goes." John rose until his head was showing above the truck and yelled, "What do you want?" and ducked just as the round whistled through the air his head had just occupied. Chet ran and dove behind the truck, his pistol in hand.

"I want a father, and right now I have decided to take him dead. You got that mister big shot rancher who abuses Mexican women and ignores his only son? You got that mister big shot rancher who thinks his big ranch and highfaluting amigos give him the right to ignore his family? Come out mister big shot rancher and let me kill you so John can go free and all will be right with the world except for me. You will be my second death from Stirrup Ranch. Billy is dead. He, the best man out here, is dead. Now I will kill you, Daddy." Miguel broke into tears of anger. It was the first time he had ever been in a position to say those words to his father. "Daddy," he sobbed, "I'm going to kill you like the rabioso perro you are. Stand up, Daddy," He spit the word, "and take it like a real man."

John looked at Chet. "That's Miguel talking. Is he really your son?"

Chet looked away, "None of your damned business."

"Chet, you are a piece of work. All we've worked so hard to accomplish with your ranch, you put all we worked for in jeopardy just because you didn't acknowledge your son. I knew you had been sleeping with Maria for a long time, but didn't know this. You, Sir, are an ass."

"Just because you own a piece of this, don't think you can get away with calling me names. I needed your money when you came along with your drug scheme, but I need it no more." Chet turned and shot the man three times.

From the brush, "Did you kill him, John? I have no beef against you."

"John is dead. It's just you and me now, you stupid kid. Do you really think a man of my stature would claim a peasant mestizo for a son? Now I will kill you and bury three bodies." He stuck his head around the back end of the truck just in time to see Miguel change positions and throw a shot from his handgun at the moving target which missed by yards.

"You had better get better at shooting, Mi Padré, or I will kill you without any danger."

Chet picked up a rifle and dug the box of ammo out of John's pocket. "Wrong caliber." He checked the chamber to make sure the gun was ready, released the safety, and prepared for war.

Miguel looked around and saw that he had put himself in a really bad position. He had no place to move to or avenue of retreat. Not that he was going anywhere, but those had always been a part of his moves in the past. The fourteen rounds he had left in his pocket would have to do the job from right where he was.

#

Aggie presented the court order to the lady at the desk in the mortuary, "Now let's get my man buried."

The woman read the document and said, "I believe there are some relatives alive somewhere. We cannot allow you to intervene even with this court order."

Aggie calmly pushed the lady aside and called the other mortuary.

A short conversation later, she looked at the woman she had pushed aside and said, "I will take my man out on the sidewalk and wait for their hearse to get here. If you try to stop me, so help me, I'll tear this place down and leave you on the bottom of the pile."

The woman sat quietly in her chair with her hands folded in her lap.

Aggie had been here before with many other folks in the back room. She had even combed her Mother's hair in the back room years ago. She marched down the hall and through a door to the right, opened the door to the chill box, and took the gurney full of her man's covered body to the back door and out to the sidewalk.

Just as she closed the door she heard, "Yes, please come quickly, she is stealing a body from our preparation room."

As Aggie stood on the sidewalk with Billy, she heard a siren start at the court house and come down the street, hardly taking two minutes to arrive in front of her.

"What are you doing, Aggie?" Deputy Art McManus said.

"Waiting for the other mortuary to get here. I have a court order allowing me to deal with Billy's body and make all the arrangements for his interment."

"May I see that, Aggie, please?"

She handed it to him.

He read it.

He said, "I'll wait right here with you so there will be no further trouble."

"Thank you, Art."

The three of them waited.

The woman inside fumed.

#

Ben handed out assignments to the deputies and sent them on their way. He and Lary headed for Stirrup Headquarters. "I'll take my truck, Crackers is more comfortable there and I can leave the working collar on him. He does not work well with strangers around."

"Sounds fair to me. Just follow me."

"I'll do that."

#

In Flagstaff two men were being held in two separate rooms at the Coconino County Sheriff's office. Deputies had worked hard all night since the truck had been found on Lake Mary Road. The drugs were under lock and key. The truck was in the impound yard. Fingerprints were being matched and the two men were very worried. The two men had been picked up on a tip from a man that had picked up two hitchhikers not a mile away from the location of the drug find. News of the find had been broadcast on the radio right after he had dropped the two walkers at a cheap motel on old 66. Before the two had even gotten to sleep, the law was at the door.

CCSO lab matched the prints and two deputies went into the first room to join the nervous suspect.

"Okay, Darrel Watson. That is your name isn't it?"

"Yeah. Why you got me here? I never done nothing wrong."

"Where's your car?"

"I sold it last week. Been walking and taking the bus since. I'm leaving this place on the first bus out after you are done with me."

"When we're done with you, you will be in prison for as long as it takes to give you a shot."

"What did I do?"

"It's simple. First, your prints are all over an old U-haul truck found full of drugs, million or so dollars' worth of drugs. Second, your buddy, what's his name?" He looked at the other Deputy.

"Lancelot Koblinski."

"Yeah, your buddy, Lance, told us you were the shooter for a murdered cop in Apache County during a drug drop."

"Not me. I don't have nothin' to do with drugs. I don't even like to take the pills the doctor orders."

The two deputies looked at each other and back to the now sweating man. "How about it? You come clean and we'll put in a good word for you. You make us work much longer and we are not going to be nice at all."

"I don't know nothin' of what you're saying. Go fly a kite. I ain't buying nothing you say."

"Okay. We'll talk to our buddy, Lance, again, and see how much he knows other that what he's told us. We'll save our good words for him."

They marched out leaving the man in a sweat under two hot lights and, as they left, turned off the air conditioning for the room.

Same routine happened in the other room. Mr. Koblinski wasn't buying what they had to sell either. He was left in his own room with the air conditioning up full blast and the one light very dim.

The two deputies went to lunch with the new young, cute stenographer who had been standing by to take the statements. She said, "I hope they break quickly, I got a hot date with a Highway Patrolman at six."

"We'll make sure it goes well into the night."

"Hey, he's my husband."

"Aw, gee. You might be late." The teasing continued.

#

One thing about an AR-15 was that even though it was not a full auto weapon, it could be fired as fast as the user could pull the trigger. Chet eased the barrel around the end of the truck, lined up the sights, and tapped the trigger three times.

Sage and dust flew up all around Miguel, but no blood was drawn. It was Miguel's turn as he lined up his own sights and eased back on the trigger while holding his breath. The gun went off and the AR-15 went spinning out of Chet's hands leaving him standing there looking at a bent barrel on the weapon lying in the dirt.

Chet rolled back toward the other rifle, the Model 70 Winchester, just as the next round went through the bed of the truck just missing him. He caught a couple pieces of metal torn from the truck by the round, blood rolled down his right arm. He flexed and checked out the arm and pronounced it good to go, which was a blessing to him due to the pain in the left from the roll over.

Chet checked the weapon and tried a few more positions which appeared to offer him better cover, but each time a round from the 7 MM whipped by dangerously close. He reached through the hole where the windshield had been and drew out a water bottle full of lukewarm water, which he downed in one motion.

Chet said to himself, "That boy is not going to let me out of here. It's him or me, and I choose for it to be him."

"Hey, Daddy. You wanna shoot it out like in the cowboy movies. I like the one with the three bad dudes standing around in a triangle, first one to draw dies. You remember, Clint Eastwood, the theme music," he imitated the whistle, "the Mexican, the gambler, and the cowboy out for revenge."

"Well, boy. You are the ugly."

"Si, I take after my padré. He is so ugly he had to settle for a Mexican woman. How could you do this to my mother? She loved you. She still does. Now she will lose both of the men she loves. I will kill you and the state will kill me. Not a good ending to the historia de amor which has lasted many years."

"I will give you half the ranch and marry Maria."

"Oh, that will make everything okay, eh? Mi Madre' gets her wedding, I get half a ranch. Oh yeah, this will make everything okay. I will have half the ranch when the gas hits me. You will be beside me for Oscar and John if you live through today. And, Mama will get the rancho for her sorrow."

"I'll hire the best attorney in the area."

Miguel laughed very loud. His ribs were hurting and he felt the ends grind together as he moved. The position he was in was not good. The condition he was in was not good. 'Things are turning not good for me at all,' he thought.

"That will be a laugh. My dead padre hiring an attorney from the grave."

He had 9 rounds left.

He put one through the truck.

#

Aggie left the Sheriff's office and out of habit turned toward the café. It was open and a couple she knew from Concho were entering. 'Time for lunch,' she thought.

Entering, she saw Maria looking very cheerful.

Maria looked to the door, "Hey, glad you are here. I have prayed and I have much comfort about Chet. My son belongs to God and He will decide how this will end. What do you want to eat?"

The man from Concho said, "Hey, we were here first."

"Oh, sorry Ted. Aggie always gets priority. We have cried together over our men."

"Well, maybe I'll wait a bit, but I am in a hurry. Gotta see the Judge today."

Aggie responded, "Won't be today. The Judge is out sick."

"How about some coffee while we wait?"

"Maria, you get the meals and I'll deal with the coffee."

"Si, that will work."

Twenty minutes later the two women left the café, after asking the Concho couple to lock the door when they left, and got in Aggie's car. "What can we do?"

"We can confront Chet with this, before the Sheriff gets him, and maybe he will do the right thing for once and give himself up, help his son, and acknowledge you as his wife."

"I don't want his ranch. I want my son."

"That might just not be possible, Maria, and you know it. He has killed."

"There were reasons."

"Maybe, but that is up to a Judge and jury. He would not get a fair trial in Apache County."

"Maybe so."

#

"Sheriff, go to channel 4."

"Sheriff, 10-4."

"Whatcha got dispatch?"

"Coconino County Sheriff is on the line. Says its extremely important."

"Patch him through."

"Sheriff Beazley, here. How's things in Coconino county, Sheriff?"

"Lousy. All your problems are becoming mine."

"How's that?"

"Got two men in my lock up."

"Yeah."

"They fessed up to hauling drugs. Named a fella that goes by the name John from Stirrup Ranch as their boss."

"Yeah. We're moving on that right now."

The Coconino Sheriff said, "Well, you might wanna hold up, I got big news for ya now."

"Wait." Ben shifted back to channel 5. "All units, hold in position until further notice." He switched back to 4 as he aimed for the shoulder of the road with his foot on the brakes.

"Okay, go ahead, Sheriff."

"Well, Ben, we went over the truck with a thin meshed net. Found all kinds of drug sign and drugs. Two bullet holes in the back of the truck just beginning to rust. The two guys in custody match prints in the truck.

"Now here's the big news. A third set of prints match a cadaver, John Doe, we have in the morgue. Died of a load of double-ought buck in the gut. Severe lead poisoning. Ain't that something, your dead in our back yard."

"That truck must have been the one used when we lost our Deputy Billings. Billings got off one round of shot. Sounds like he did something right after all. I thought we had that man over in the morgue at the Show Low Hospital. There must have been an empty in his shotgun we missed."

"There are two more sets of prints we were able to pick up. I'll fax them to you."

"Put them in a cruiser and send them if you will. I'll owe ya. Can't do nothing with faxed prints. I'll have a person meet ya at the Navajo County line. That work for you?"

"Yeah. We are still grilling these two. Will keep ya posted."

"Thanks, take care."

"Dispatch."

"Yes, Sheriff."

Ben outlined the need of the prints and the way to get them to him quickly, county to county to county to him.

It was not two minutes later when, "Sheriff, Dispatch. Roy Carson is on the line, patching him through on 4."

"Wait, don't."

"Too late."

"What do you want, Roy?"

"Got a dealer for you. Taped the buy. Got lots of samples."

"I need another dealer like I need another hole in my head. Who is it?"

"Pony Boy Yashtee."

"Oh, fiddlesticks. Not Ms. Willa Yashtee's kid?"

"No, Ben. Her husband."

Lary had stopped behind Ben and was now tapping on the passenger side window. Ben rolled the electric window down.

"Hang on, Lary."

"Roy, you're telling me you got the goods on Ms. Yastee's husband?"

"Yup."

"Give the evidence to Diane and go write your story, but do not publish yet."

"10-4 out.

"Diane, you got anybody else on the phone."

"Not for you, boss."

"Back to 5."

"Channel 5. Everybody hold, please. Smoke'em if ya got'em."

Ben clued Lary in on the new developments.

Lary said, "What difference does it make? We bust Chet and John, figure out which one's running the show and then take them to court. We get Miguel, his case is in the bag. Sounds like you have all the suspects you need on Deputy Billing's death, even two with your brand of shot in his dead belly. So, why hold?"

"Mr. Ronson, it's just my style."

A car went passed them. Ben said, "Aggie, must be going to Holbrook for the court or something to do with Billy's funeral. I'm not looking forward to the aftermath of all this. Chet's next of kin is Miguel. Miguel's next of kin is Maria. Billy has no next of kin. Closest to him is Aggie. Billy had no will. This is a pile of crap ten feet deep and I don't have the energy to shovel."

"Let's take it one problem at a time. Let's bust Chet and John. Then we can find Miguel. Coconino has the other three. You can transport. "

On the radio, "Sheriff."

"Yes, Diane, who is it this time?"

"Coconino Sheriff reports both suspects have clammed up and demanded a lawyer."

"Tell him, I will get warrants and extradite soonest."

"10-4."

"Well, Mr. Ronson, onward and upward, let's go whup somebody."

"I'm all for it. I hate drugs."

"I hate crime."

"Touché."

"You wanna ride with me?"

"Nope. Back to my dog."

"Let's go then."

#

Miguel could feel the blood running into his pants. His shirt was soaked, but it was all he had. He wadded the body part of the shirt into as small a ball as possible and laid it over the wound, wrapped the sleeves around his waist, and tied it as tight as possible. It even felt better.

#

Chet looked around noting avenues of escape were few. He stuck Johns S&W up over the bed and fired twice. No response. The Model 70 was his next shot from the front of the truck letting him have the engine between Miguel and his body. Nothing.

The gas spilling at the back of the truck made him not want to do any shooting from that end. The sand and brush was sucking up the liquid like it was water. Chet feared shooting in that area. He didn't want the muzzle flash or a spark to ignite his hiding spot.

He noticed that the hood was sprung a bit. Pulling on it he achieved a hole through the engine compartment. It took a bit of effort, but he was able to get the Model 70 in a position for a line of sight directly at Miguel without exposing himself too much. Lining the sights up, he waited.

#

"Okay, boys and girls. Let's do this. All units to assigned places." He didn't want to say much, even on channel 5. There was always some nut with a scanner on everything. Or, the crooks might have used some of their gains to purchase the best.

#

Miguel noticed a rooster tail of dust coming up the road into the ranch. He could not see a vehicle, but assumed it was the law. 'My time is getting shorter by the minute,' he thought.

He watched a rifle barrel move into action at the front of the truck. Through the scope he could see the front sight and down to the forestock. The hole in the barrel was pointed directly at his position.

#

Lary saw the rooster tail moving in the direction of Stirrup and grumbled under his breath. "Somebody is getting in the way."

From the way Ben was shaking his head in the car ahead of him, Lary knew that Ben was thinking what he was, 'this could mean trouble.'

Crackers left the floor and climbed onto the seat on the passenger's side and began looking out of the window, giving a low growl.

"That's right, boy, more people in the mix. I just hope that Chet is not entertaining today. A mess of people would really get in the way.

#

Chet saw the rooster tail and figured somebody was joining the party and he did not want any gate crashers. He looked back along the sights and swore, "Just stick that dirty brown nose of yours out, punk. I'll take it off."

As if in answer, a head came into view. He squeezed the trigger.

The head disappeared.

#

Miguel pulled back the fist just in time to have the round from Chet's gun miss by less than an inch. He waited a few moments and tried it again. Again, Chet missed. 'Game time is over.'

He put three quick shots through the hood of the truck.

The third shot brought a scream from Chet and the barrel of the gun sticking out of the truck pointed up and slid back through the hole.

Miguel cried. He had killed his father.

He yelled, "You hit?"

No response.

He stood, carefully watching the barrel sticking out of the truck.

He took a step or two toward his target.

Miguel walked to the truck and around the back of it. Chet was laying in the dirt facing away, one hand under his chest, his legs contorted, and the other hand full of dirt. Miguel prodded the body with the barrel of his rifle before walking up and, with a toe under the hip, rolled Chet over.

Chet's arm came up with a stubby automatic and put three rounds that could have been covered by a half-dollar in Miguel's heart.

His son fell in the dirt like all his bones had melted, just a twisted pile of human tissue and bone at his feet. Chet Handley kicked him. And, again. Screamed. Kicked again.

And, started walking to the ranch house.

#

Aggie heard three spaced shots.

"Somebody is shooting up something or someone."

Moments later, three rapid shots filled the air.

"Somebody is still alive."

Maria cried, "Miguel is dead, I feel it."

"You cannot know."

"I know he is dead. Chet lives."

Aggie pulled up next to the house. They both left the car and carried their purses.

Maria asked, "Why do we need our purses? Is it just habit?"

"Yeah, just habit." She was reassured by the weight of hers.

#

Chet pulled a small tube from his pocket, unscrewed the lid, shook out a match, lit it, and, as he walked away, tossed the burning match onto the gas damp ground. The truck went up in a flash, with the heat blast knocking him down. Chet scrambled to his feet and looked over the scene. The body of Miguel was at the edge of the pool of fuel. As he watched, his son's clothes began to burn. He started moving toward the house, running, carrying only the S & W.

"Where can I go? Where can I hide?" he asked the wind.

#

Maria heard the woosh of the fire and turned. "Aggie, look! Something has exploded. Look at the fireball. An oil or gas fire looks like a small atom bomb."

The two of them watched, mesmerized, until they could see a man running toward them.

"Who is it?"

"It is not my Miguel. It is too skinny for John. It is Chet. Miguel is dead, just like I told you."

The two women started toward the man. Aggie opened her purse and tucked the .45 behind her waistband at the small of her back. She watched Maria stop, drop her purse, and fall to her knees.

"It's Chet," Aggie said. "I will not have to confront the son." She began plodding to her friend.

#

Chet was not over a hundred yards away when he saw the two women. Maria started toward him. "Damn." He trotted slower. The thoughts that ran through his head were not good ones. The owner of the biggest ranch in the area, the richest man in the county, the murderer, the drug dealer, the only son of an only son had come to a point in life where all the sticks fell in such a way he could not pick up one of them.

"All I can do is lie."

As he neared the woman on her knees, he said, "Maria, John killed our son. I have killed John. Will you marry me? I love you."

Maria stopped cold in the middle of her prayers. Looking up, she saw the man who set her on fire for years, who had lied to her for years, who had caused the death of the son of her love. "You are an ugly man. I do not know what I ever saw in you, Chet Handley. You are a self-centered, selfish, ugly man. I would die before I would marry you."

She stood, turned, and started walking back to Aggie who was standing, frozen in the shock of the words she had heard from her friend.

Chet stopped. Lifted the hand with the gun and said, "You will never marry anyone. I will kill you as I killed him. A wetback woman and mestizo son could never be a part of my life, my heart, my dreams. You were just an easy girl who became an easy woman." He started walking again with the gun in his outstretched hand.

Aggie yelled, "Look out, Maria. He has a gun pointed right at you."

Maria turned, raised her arms, and said, "Here I am, still an easy target for a man like you. Use me again to vent your rage at being found out. Liar! Killer! Drug Lord! I have no feeling but pity for you."

Chet saw another car followed by an old, partly green pickup truck entering the yard. He knew it was over. All he had left was to run. But, before he ran, he had one more thing to do. His second arm swung up with the hand wrapping around the other. He stopped and posted himself as if he were on a target range.

"Maria, drop." The voice was that of Lary who was standing at the door of his truck with the M-16 laid across the window sill aimed at Chet's head.

Ben yelled, "Chet, drop the gun in the name of the law. I have a warrant for your arrest, duly signed by the Judge. There are Deputies coming in from every access there is to this ranch. You are busted. It's all over. Drop. The. Gun." The last three words were said in a tone that left no doubt he meant it.

"Go away. I will take Maria with me. He moved quickly toward the woman, keeping her in Lary's line of sight.

Aggie screamed, "I'll kill you. It was you who caused Billy's death. It was you who killed the only joy Maria had. I will kill you."

Chet turned to look at her and watched as she pulled the large revolver from her waistband, bring it around front, and struggle to lift it with both hands.

"Drop, Aggie," Ben yelled.

"Drop, Maria," Lary yelled.

Aggie struggled to get the hammer back, until it clicked into firing position so loudly that all five of them heard it.

Chet swung to bring her in his sight pattern just as she pulled the trigger.

Chet folded in the middle.

Click. Click.

She pulled the trigger again.

The round went in between his shoulder blades and destroyed his spine.

Chet fell like a bag of rags and rolled backwards a few feet, coming to rest with his face buried in his chest, his heart pumping out the last of his blood on the ground he had struggled to hold. Now he would be buried in it.

Maria fell to her knees again and began praying for his soul.

Aggie dropped the big gun and began crying.

Lary ran to Chet's body to make sure he was dead, although he had no doubts, but his training led the way.

Ben stood next to his car with his mouth open watching the tableau before him until finally, he reached in and picked up the mike. "Dispatch. I need the ME, two ambulances, and that's all out here at Stirrup headquarters. All units stand down except 8, 6, and 2 who will report to me at the ranch house."

"10-4."

"2 ten minutes out."

"6 coming up behind you."

"8 is stopped on the road from Homestead Well at a fire. There is a truck burning and what looks like two bodies in the flames on the ground. Request fire units, ambulance, and backup."

"12 back up 8. Dispatch get fire units out here also. That fire is just outta sight of Stirrup. Juan keep going past us, go way around us, and follow the road to Homestead. Backup 8 until 12 gets there."

"10-4. Moving around you now."

All was quiet for the time it took Juan to go around and reach the two rut road again. As he topped the rise, a saddled horse caught his attention. It was Tonio's horse standing patiently over a body. Juan yelled on the mike, "Got a body out here by a horse. Looks like Tonio." There was a pause. "It is Tonio. He is still alive, but just barely. Ben, can you get someone else to help 8?"

Chapter 17

The next morning the Board of Supervisors met very early. They ordered the Sheriff to attend the afternoon session using Ms. Yashtee as the messenger. She caught up with Ben in the Café eating his breakfast after leaving the scene at Stirrup in the hands of three fresh deputies. Maria was doing a fine job this morning of loading everything with green peppers and Ben was having trouble getting enough milk to put out the fire.

"I will talk with you, Sheriff?"

He stood, "Please join me. Would you like some coffee or maybe even one of these wonderful green chili omelets?"

"This is not social, Sheriff. I want your badge. Yellowtail wants your badge. We demand that you be at the Supervisor's meeting at 1 PM. You know the location."

"You demand?"

"Yes."

"Was this unanimous?"

"There was no vote. Mr. Yellowtail and I are running this county now. Your Mr. Hardesty no longer has any power. We control the vote. We control it all."

"I'm sorry to hear that, Ms. Yashtee."

"I'll just bet you are. If you aren't, you will be."

"Yes, Ma'am. You see I will be by your reservation at Pine Springs in no less that 90 minutes for a social visit. I should be back in St. Johns by 2 PM barring the unforeseen."

"Why are you visiting my town, Mr. Beazley.?"

"I cannot tell you that at this time. I will be happy to explain around three this afternoon if that meets your schedule and approval."

"I will see you at three in the Board Room."

"Very well. Have a nice day, Ms. Yashtee."

#

Juan sat at the side of Tonio in the Show Low Hospital looking at his young relative. "How's the pain?"

"It is no worse than getting kicked in the back by a caballo with iron shoes. I have been hurt mas malo. What do the medico says?"

Juan looked him in the eye, "The doctor says you will never be able to have children, no ninos. And, your sister will marry me."

"I will never allow such a thing for my sister. It is my shoulder so the ninos are still in the future." He smiled at the way Juan looked after he spoiled his joke. "My shoulder and arm, what is to become of them."

"They will be there for many years to come, says the doctor. But, there will be at least one more operation to rebuild your shoulder bone and collar bone. You are still the lucky one. Nothing vital was hit. He says you will be as good as an old man with that arm in no time."

"I feel like the old man now."

"You will live to make strong sons and they will be better cowboys than their father."

"I will ask for nothing more, that will make them damn fine vaqueros."

Tonio fell asleep.

Juan went home to sleep. He had not had sleep since early yesterday.

#

"Dispatch, have Deputy Connor meet me at the Houck turnoff of I-40 in one hour."

"10-4, Sheriff."

#

Lary Ronson sat on his front porch watching the sun rise drinking cowboy coffee out of a blue tin cup that had been poured from a blue tin pot. He had been sitting in the same place since an hour before the sun broke over the eastern horizon. It was now high enough that the sun itself was blocked by the overhanging porch roof.

Crackers was working through the sage and snake weed looking for anything that would run so he could give chase. The dog's fur shined in the sun emphasizing the black and the small spots of white on her chest.

"Crackers, we need to get to town," he paused, "or do we?" The dog came to the voice of his master. "Why? I don't know. They will need no more from us until the trials, which will be months from now. Let's go tell Phoenix, we quit. It's time to retire."

Crackers thumped his tail on the porch planking and ran for the truck.

"Not now, dog. How about tomorrow? Or, maybe the next day?"

#

Aggie looked like she felt as she walked through the door of the café. "Maria, I need coffee, por favor."

"You need more than coffee. You look terrible. Are you sick?"

"I have not slept."

"Por qué?"

"I killed a man. I never thought I could or would do that. I killed a man." She began crying, again.

"You save my life and maybe Sheriff Ben's or Señor Ronson's. We could have all been killed if you had not kill Chet. I know he was money hungry, but I did not think he was mucho malo. You save my life. He kill my son, his son. He kill John, maybe so. He shoot Tonio, or have John do it, we don't know. How many he kill or ruin with his drugs? How many, Mi Amiga? How many?" She, too, cried.

Maria had slowly walked toward Aggie as she talked and when she finished talking, she wrapped her arms around Aggie and the two of them cried together in the middle of the room.

Not a customer commented. Lew left his wife in the booth and began serving coffee to the customers Maria could not serve for a few minutes. Sue got up and checked with each busy table to see if they had a need. Everyone in the place was cared for.

Finally, Maria led Aggie to an empty booth and sat her down. "I am sorry it was you. More better the law. What will you have to eat, Aggie? On the house. Then we will go to the church and light candles."

#

Bud woke up to find the bed beside him empty. He pulled on his pants as he searched the house. Carrie was sitting at the dining table drinking tea with a big smile on her face.

"I was worried about you," he said.

"I got tired of the bed. My bed sores were getting sores."

"You don't have bed sores," he said, "do you?"

"No, silly. I am the Mommy here and I will run my own kitchen. My daughter will go to camp next week. My son with get in shape for the two-a-days the coach will require shortly. We will be a family of joy again."

"But, the doctor told you . . ."

"Piffle, I will not stay in that bed. I will go slow and easy. The kids will help. You will go back to work and make the money to help the rest of this mob through college if they wish to go. You want coffee or tea?"

"Coffee."

She stood slowly, moved to the coffee maker, returned with the carafe, and poured into the mug he always used which she had already set on the table. "There you are, my husband. I love you."

"And I love you more than I can ever put into words or actions."

"I know," she said with a twist of a smile on her lips.

#

At 3 PM Ben Beazley walked into the Board Room, smiled, and sat down in the audience seats.

"Sheriff, will you please come to the front table," Mr. Yellowtail asked. He smirked as he finished the request.

"I would be happy to."

Ms. Yashtee said to the crowd, "We will now go into executive session to deal with personnel matters. Thank you all for coming and please leave in an orderly manner."

The Board waited until all except the three of them, the Sheriff, the County Manager, the County Attorney, and the backup recorder were left in the room.

Mel Hardesty jumped in first, "Ben, I have no say, but I support you."

"Thanks, Mel. I understand." He took off his hat and looked down at his boots. 'Dang, they need polishing again,' he thought.

"Well, Sheriff, welcome to our Board Room."

"I didn't come here for stupid comments like that. Get on with it." He figured he would set the tone of this confrontation and not her.

Ms. Yashtee said, "Sheriff, you have been and are a waste of money. Crime runs rampant throughout the county."

"Yeah, and its three times as bad on the Reservation."

"Stop. I will tell you when you may talk."

"Whoa, right there, Yellowtail. I am elected just like you. You have no authority over me unless you have a felony to convict me of, and then DPS and the Court are the ones I talk to."

Willa Yashtee leaned over the dais and stuck her finger out, "You have let the dopers, the rustlers, the destroyers of property run freely throughout this county. You will not work with the Navajo Police. You are a belligerent and overly proud man who collects his paycheck and does nothing but sit in his office smoking cheap cigars, or hangs out in Lenny's Place with the riffraff of the area."

"Are you finished with your hateful spiel yet?" He smiled at the Board. "I have something to say before you both make fools of yourselves."

"Speak." She screamed the word.

"The killers of Oscar Billings are in jail or dead. The rustlers and their truckers are in jail. The shooter is dead. The main drug dealer is dead, as is his partner and two of his workers. Two drug dealers are in jail. The killer of Barto is dead. The crime spree is over. I even issued a parking ticket this morning on your truck, Mr. Yellowtail, you are too close to the crosswalk. And, Ms. Yastee, your husband was arrested this morning in Pine Springs with over 20 pounds of marijuana and at least a hundred dime bags of Meth. We have him cold. Selling on tape and samples of his weed matches the stuff dropped when Oscar was killed. I am sorry to say we cannot put him at the scene. The only person we don't have is the pilot of the plane and his plane. Thank you for the opportunity to bring you up to date on the situation in Apache County."

He turned and walked out, followed by all those present except the two, in control, supervisors.

He kicked himself mentally again. Oscar had been a good enough man to get two on the runway. One empty shell was found there and the other was found in his shotgun. He died with the second shot and never jacked in a new round.

#

Artie lifted his suitcase into the luggage compartment and went back to the office to file his flight plan for his first trip in his own plane, destination Alaska.

If you liked this book,
check out Doug's other books at
www.amazon.com/author/dougball

Try the State of Arizona series
including

STATE OF DEFENSE #1
STATE OF THREAT #2

Or, the westerns

BLOOD ON THE ZUNI
VENGEANCE

Patti thinks that
GENTLE REBELLION
is the best of Doug's books,
but she's prejudice.